CARICOM GCC: Syncretic Visionaries in Paradise

Caribbean Paradisiacal Places, Volume 2

DR. RAONA REFIT

Published by R.E.F.I.T PUBLISHING, 2025.

This is a work of fiction. Similarities to real people, places, or events are entirely coincidental.

CARICOM GCC: SYNCRETIC VISIONARIES IN PARADISE

First edition. January 6, 2025.

ISBN: 978-1068655821

Written by DR. RAONA REFIT.

Table of Contents

Table of Contents

An inspirational dedication to all readers who are:

Ambitious innovators developing healthy recipes of entrepreneurism.

Talented dreamers successfully actualizing syncretic connections.

Peaceful futurists aiming to harmonize, unite and exemplify cultural empowerment.

A Entrepreneurial Fusion of CARICOM and GCC Visionaries: Honoring Heritage, Dreaming Big, Illustrating how Historical Wanderlust Weaves Tales of Trade and Tradition, Syncretizing Cultures

CARICOM GCC:
Syncretic Visionaries in Paradise
Artistically and Entrepreneurially Driven
Novelette Part 1 – The Gulf-Caribbean Memoirs: Trade and Travels
Novelette Part 2 – A Culinary Cookbook of Friendships, Heritage, and Entrepreneurial Connections

The first part of this novelette, set over archival times between Caribbean and Arab populations uncovers memoirs of family and friendship connections. Each chapter educates the reader on cultural history and traditions while immersing you into the lives of generations of artistic visionaries and entrepreneurs documenting their dreams and telling tales of world adventures and achievements while syncretizing their heritage and ideas with class and emboldened endeavours.

It aims to enlighten you in different languages, evoke your culinary senses and sets out to provide further exploration of CARICOM and GCC countries during modern times, through the sharing of different flavours and contemporary topical events in the heartwarming and inspiring second part of the novelette. Building on elements from the previous, narratives are enhanced with a broader scope, deeper character development, and a stronger emphasis on cultural exchange and the power of food to connect people across continents.

A cookbook of culinary delights is revealed highlighting innovative cultural exchange, and the enduring power and impact of family and friendships. Chapters reveal recipes to celebrate culinary diversity, providing a delicious invitation to explore the Caribbean and Arab worlds, through different fusion flavours each time.

Chapter 1: The Traders' Visions

R amar, a young boy with eyes the colour of the Arabian glowing sands and a heart brimming with love and curiosity, was fascinated by his grandfather's world. The labyrinthine souq, a kaleidoscope of sights and sounds, was his playground. He knew the secret passages of each stall alleyway, the subtle nuances of each spice flowing through the air – the fiery bite of chilli, the earthy warmth of cumin, the delicate sweetness of cardamom. The midday sun beat down on Deira, baking the cobblestones into a shimmering haze. Dust sparkles danced in the distance, swirling across an array of shops. Young Ramar, his brow damp with sweat, hurried through the bustling souq as the aroma of spices and exotic perfumes filled his nostrils. He carried a small sack of the best saffron, evidence of the new business deal struck between his Emirati grandfather the renowned spice merchant of Old Dubai and this new, yet already famous Omani trader, Salim.

Ramar's grandfather, Omar, was an Emirati with Saudi heritage and a local legend in Deira. His spice shop, a haven of fragrant aromas, was a gathering place for merchants, visitors, and locals alike. Omar, with his flowing beard and eyes that twinkled with wisdom, possessed a knowledge of spices passed down through generations. He could identify the quality of any spice by its mere scent, and his skills were renowned throughout the region.

Salim, a seasoned trader from Muscat, had arrived in this burgeoning coastal village a few months ago, drawn by whispers of opportunity. Deira, though a fledgling settlement compared to the grander ports of the Persian Gulf, possessed a raw energy, a place of adventure that resonated deeply with the Omani in him. Salim enjoyed mentoring younger traders from all over the Arabian Peninsula, sharing his wisdom and experience. He wanted to instil in them the pride for his region, values of honesty, integrity, and a deep respect for the Arabian sea and its unpredictable nature. He wanted to infuse the importance of building relationships, of fostering trust and understanding among the diverse communities that inhabited the shores of the Gulf. Therefore, when Ramar, the grandson of one of the most well-known Emirati traders, with an entrepreneurial spirit came into his new shop and wanted to know about his reputation, he naturally shared his talents. He had a vision for the tenacity of Omani traders to be spread far and wide. Salim wanted his legacy to spread beyond Oman sharing the spirit of enterprise, the interconnectedness of trade, the respect for cultural exchange to flourish all over the world. Hence it was a pleasure to share his adventures and successes with Ramar.

Salim's successes extended far beyond his own country. As an accomplished trader he had not only introduced the exquisite flavours of Oman to the people of Deira but had also played a crucial role in fostering economic growth and cultural exchange in the region. The vibrant hues of saffron, once a distant dream, now adorned the tables of the wealthy and the plates of the common folk, a testament to his vision and perseverance in daring to venture beyond the horizon and bring the treasures of his homeland to the shores of the Persian Gulf.

In Deira, saffron quickly became a sensation. It was used to infuse rice dishes with a golden hue and an intoxicating aroma. It lent a subtle sweetness to delicate pastries and a touch of elegance to savoury stews. Wealthy merchants, seeking to impress their guests, adorned their tables with dishes infused with the precious spice. But the allure of saffron extended beyond the culinary realm. It was highly prized for its medicinal properties. Local healers and apothecaries recognized its therapeutic value. Saffron was believed to have calming properties, to aid digestion, and to improve eyesight. It was used to treat a variety of ailments, from headaches to insomnia.

The arrival of the Portuguese in the early 16th century had thrown the delicate balance of trade in the Gulf into disarray. Their imposing galleons, bristling with cannons, had disrupted established routes, extorting exorbitant taxes from weary merchants. The once-vibrant trade networks, painstakingly woven by generations of Omani seafarers, lay in tatters.

Salim's life and family history was not without its trials. He grew up around his elders explaining how they weathered storms that threatened to sink their dhows, faced the wrath of rival merchants, and endured the ever-present threat of piracy. Yet, through it all, they persevered, driven by an unwavering entrepreneurial spirit and a deep-seated belief in the enduring strength of the Omani trading tradition. Like many other Omani traders, they refused to succumb to Portuguese dominance. As countrymen, resourceful and resilient, they sought out alternative routes, navigating treacherous waters and forging new alliances with local tribes. They traded in whispers, their voices hushed, their cargo concealed beneath layers of fish and dried dates.

Life under Portuguese rule was a constant game of cat and mouse. Salim's forefathers, with keen understanding of the shifting winds of fortune and an uncanny ability to anticipate the Portuguese moves, thrived. As a result, their gifts passed onto him and Salim built a reputation for his integrity, his word as good as gold in the bustling souqs of Deira.

The 17th century brought a glimmer of hope he went on to explain to Ramar. The Portuguese grip on the Gulf began to weaken, their power gradually eroding under the relentless pressure of local resistance and shifting alliances. Omani traders expanded their operations, venturing further afield, his dhows laden with precious cargo – silks from India, spices from the East Indies, and the coveted pearls of the Gulf.

The rise of the Yarubid Dynasty in Oman in the 18th century ushered in a new era of Omani maritime dominance. Salim, buoyed by this resurgence and born of this time, grew to build on the operations of his family trade. They invested in larger dhows, employing skilled craftsmen to build vessels that could withstand the rigors of long voyages. Their trading routes stretched across the Indian Ocean, reaching as far as Zanzibar and the East African coast. The influx of goods from across the Indian Ocean spread and they transformed the local economy of Deira, Old Dubai, introducing new flavours, new fabrics, and new ideas. The town began to take on a cosmopolitan character, a melting pot of cultures and traditions.

However, the 19th century brought new challenges. The British, seeking to expand their influence in the region, posed a formidable competitor to Omani traders. Salim, a wise man by now, ever adaptable, navigated this new landscape with a shrewd blend of competition and cooperation. He established trade agreements with British merchants, recognizing the inevitability of their growing presence, while simultaneously seeking to protect his own interests and those of his fellow Omani traders.

The thriving trading post in Oman that his family had developed became a meeting place for merchants from all over the Arab world, a hub of information and exchange. Over time with an extensive network of historical contacts across the region, Salim became a vital link, connecting the disparate communities that dotted the coastline. Obtaining saffron was no easy feat. The delicate crimson threads, painstakingly extracted from the Crocus sativus flower, were cultivated in limited quantities in the highlands of Oman. Salim spent months cultivating relationships with the local farmers, offering them fair prices and ensuring the highest quality saffron. He learned the nuances of saffron cultivation, understanding the importance of soil, climate, and meticulous harvesting techniques.

His journeys between Oman and Deira were regularly fraught with peril. Pirates roamed the seas, ever vigilant for unsuspecting merchant vessels. However, by now Salim, was a seasoned mariner. He knew the routes and employed wise tactics to evade pirate attacks, utilizing the knowledge of local currents and the expertise of his seasoned crew.

Whenever news of Salim's arrival laden with the finest saffron from Oman reached Dubai, it spread like wildfire through the market. Merchants, intrigued by the vibrant crimson threads and their alluring aroma, flocked to Salim's trading post. Salim, a master storyteller, knew how to captivate his audience. He spoke of the intricate process of saffron cultivation, of the delicate dance between sun and shadow, and of the skilled hands that plucked the delicate flowers. He described the myriad uses of saffron, not only as a culinary delight but also as a revered medicinal herb.

Salim, recognizing the potential of saffron as both a culinary delight and a valuable medicinal herb, began to educate the local community about its uses. He organized cooking demonstrations, showcasing the versatility of saffron in various dishes. He also collaborated with local healers, sharing his knowledge of traditional Omani medicinal practices that incorporated saffron.

News about Salim's saffron spread far beyond Deira. Merchants from other parts of the Gulf, intrigued by its exceptional quality, began to seek out Salim's wares. His new Deira trading post soon became a hub of activity, a meeting place for merchants from across the region. Ever the astute businessman, he understood the importance of building lasting relationships with those around him. He treated his customers with respect, offering fair prices and ensuring their satisfaction. He cultivated trust and loyalty, building a strong network of clients who came to rely on him for the finest saffron in the region. As his business flourished, Salim continued to explore new avenues, always seeking to expand his horizons. He wanted to venture into other lucrative trades, such as the pearl trade, while maintaining his focus on the saffron trade. He knew that Omar, one of the best local Emirati spice traders had great connections with pearl traders and had family and friends who were excellent artisans and craftsmen, contributing to the overall prosperity of the community.

Ramar listened, yearning to know what could be beyond his grandfather's shop. He dreamt of faraway lands, of bustling ports and exotic markets, of the whispers of the wind carrying tales of distant shores. He longed to see the world beyond the dusty walls of Deira, to experience the wonders that lay beyond the horizon.

When arriving at his grandfather's shop to deliver Salim's saffron, Ramar stumbled upon a hidden compartment within a large wooden chest. Inside, nestled amongst fragrant bundles of herbs, lay a worn leather-bound journal. Its pages, filled with elegant Arabic script, spoke of 'rihlat khatira' across the seas, of the dangerous journeys that could be encountered with pirates and sultans, of a life far removed from the familiar rhythms of Deira. The journal belonged to his great-grandfather, a daring adventurer who had sailed the Silk Road, trading spices and silks with merchants from distant lands. Ramar was captivated because his grandfather had also added to the journal.

Chapter 2: The Journal Becomes the Journey

A s Ramar read he devoured the journal, his imagination soaring with every word. He read of his great-grandfather's introduction to pearl and spice trading. He learned of his great-grandfather's encounters with different cultures, his fascination with their customs and traditions, and his unwavering pursuit of new flavours and experiences.

The journal spoke of a world beyond his wildest imagination, a world filled with adventure, discovery, and the thrill of the unknown. As Ramar delved deeper into his great-grandfather's captivating tales, his own dreams of exploration began to take shape. He followed his grandfather's writings of wanting to venture beyond the known world, of discovering new lands and new flavours, and of adding his own chapter to the family's legacy of trading and cultural exploration.

Omar's ambitions extended beyond simply trading. He yearned for knowledge, for a deeper understanding of the world and its diverse cultures. He dreamt of expanding his horizons, developing others within his community, venturing beyond the known world, of experiencing different ways of life and learning from other civilizations. He was a man of insatiable curiosity, spent countless hours poring over ancient maps, their faded inks whispering tales of forgotten empires and legendary voyages. He carefully traced the Silk Road, imagining caravans laden with silks, spices, and precious stones winding their way across the vast expanse of Asia. He studied the intricate navigational charts of Arab astronomers, their knowledge of the stars guiding sailors across the treacherous seas.

He frequented the bustling harbour, where seasoned sailors spun tales of their voyages. He listened intently to their stories of encounters with exotic creatures, of navigating treacherous storms, and of discovering hidden coves and uncharted islands. He wrote about one old sailor, with eyes that held the wisdom of a thousand voyages, spoke of a land far to the west, a land of untold riches and unimaginable wonders. He described lush terrains teeming with life, rivers flowing with precious minerals, and spices that grew in abundance – cinnamon, nutmeg, and vanilla, the likes of which Omar had never even imagined.

This mythical land, shrouded in mystery and whispered about in hushed tones, piqued Omar's curiosity. He devoured every word, his imagination ignited by the sailor's vivid descriptions. He envisioned a land of vibrant colours and intoxicating aromas, a land where spices grew in abundance, a land where he could discover new flavours and expand his knowledge of the world. This encounter with the seasoned sailor became a turning point for Omar. He realized that the world was far larger than he had ever imagined, a vast and interconnected tapestry of cultures and experiences. He decided that he would not be content to remain within the confines of Deira. He yearned to explore the unknown, to experience the world firsthand, and to bring back not only exotic spices but also a wealth of knowledge and understanding.

He began to intensely research the 'Ealam Jadid' studying the accounts of explorers who had dared to venture across the vast ocean to this 'New World'. He learned of the intricate trade routes that connected Europe to the Americas, of the exchange of goods and ideas that had shaped the world. He envisioned a journey that would not only expand his spice trade but also enrich his understanding of the world, forging connections between civilizations and fostering a deeper appreciation for human diversity.

Omar, a man of vision and ambition, began to prepare for his journey. He gathered provisions – dried dates, sacks of rice, barrels of water, and a treasure trove of spices. He also collected a variety of goods to trade along the way – fine silks from Persia, intricate jewellery from India, and exquisite carpets from the heart of the Ottoman Empire. He assembled a crew of skilled sailors and experienced traders, men who shared his passion for exploration and his thirst for knowledge.

And this is where the journal ended – the journey never materialised. It was at this moment that Ramar was destined to make sure it would!

Omar had meticulously annotated the map, marking potential trading routes and potential points of interest. Ramar, his eyes wide with wonder, traced the route with his finger, sought knowledge from all the traders who came from far and wide, the bustling bazaars of Oman, to the stalls of Ottoman lands and Indian subcontinent, and the mysterious lands beyond the western horizon. He learned from traders like Salim about the monsoon winds, the stars that guided sailors across the vast ocean, and the importance of forging alliances with local traders. He even began to learn basic phrases in Arabic, eager to communicate with the people he would encounter on his travels. He asked which stars were the most important to follow, "*Ramar anzur 'iilaa najm alshamal*", 'ahh yes' he thought remembering this from his teacher at school – 'The North Star is always the brightest'. He made sure to remember "*kayf haluk?*" when greeting anyone on his journey because he knew the importance of being polite and showing interest in how someone is.

Omar, noticing Ramar's growing fascination with the journal and his burgeoning desire for adventure, encouraged his grandson's passion in every way he could. He spent countless hours with Ramar, sharing his vast knowledge of spices. He taught him to identify the subtle nuances of each spice, from the fiery bite of chilli to the delicate sweetness of cardamom, by simply inhaling their aroma. He imparted the secrets of his most prized spice blends, each a unique symphony of flavours, passed down through generations of his family.

He also instilled in Ramar the importance of building relationships with trusted traders. "Trust is the foundation of any successful venture," Omar would often say. "*kun mhtrman wsadqan*", Ramar would repeat it over and over: 'koon muh-tar-a-man wa sa-dee-qan' to never forget that he needed to be honest and respectful with everyone he met along the way. Omar would nod approvingly and continue to teach Ramar skills in the art of negotiation, the importance of listening attentively, and the value of building long-lasting relationships with his trading partners.

Omar shared stories of his own adventures, of the bustling bazaars of Istanbul, of the vibrant colours of the Indian subcontinent, and of the mysterious lands beyond the western horizon. He spoke of the challenges he had faced – treacherous storms, fierce competition, and the ever-present threat of pirates. But he also spoke of the triumphs, of the joy of forging unexpected friendships, and of the thrill of exploring the unknown. He emphasized the importance of perseverance, resilience, and the pursuit of knowledge. He would remind Ramar that the world is a vast and ever-changing place, pointing out that true adventurers must be adaptable, resourceful, and always eager to learn. He encouraged Ramar to embrace the unknown, to step outside his comfort zone, and most importantly *'taealam lughatahum'.* Ramar would come to realise that it truly was vital to 'learn the language' of the land he would explore.

These lessons of guidance, imparted with love and wisdom, resonated deeply with Ramar. He began to see the world through his grandfather's eyes, as a place of endless possibilities, a canvas upon which to paint his own unique story. He spent hours studying maps, tracing the routes his grandfather had taken, imagining the sights, sounds, and smells of the exotic lands he had encountered. He learned about the winds and currents, the stars and the constellations, preparing himself for the day when he too would embark on his own voyage of discovery.

The shadow of mortality, ever present in the lives of all men, began to fall upon Omar. His once vibrant spirit began to wane, his step losing its spring. One evening, as they sat together in the spice shop,

Omar, his voice hoarse but filled with a lifetime of wisdom, told Ramar, "*kun shujaean*," and in turn Ramar repeated it 'koon shoo-ja-an'. Omar wanted to ensure his grandson remembered to 'be brave' and embrace the unknown fearlessly with joy for the adventures. And then, with a gentle sigh, Omar calmy slipped away, leaving behind a profound silence in the spice shop. Ramar, grief-stricken but determined, vowed to honour his grandfather's legacy. He would not allow fear to deter him from his dreams. He would embark on his own voyage of discovery, carrying with him the spirit of his grandfather, the wisdom of his teachings, and the legacy of a family dedicated to the pursuit of knowledge and the exploration of the world.

As Ramar grew older, his desire to embark on his own voyage of discovery intensified. He spent years studying navigation charts, learning the art of celestial navigation, and honing his skills as a trader. He built a network of contacts, establishing relationships with merchants across the region. He even began to invest in a small fleet of dhows, preparing for the day when he would finally set sail on his own grand adventure.

This was in 1864, a time of unprecedented change and upheaval in the Ottoman Empire. The once formidable empire and neighbouring Arab region was facing growing internal strife and external pressures. Yet, amidst the growing unease, Ramar's spirit remained undiminished. He believed that exploration and cultural exchange were more important than ever, that by connecting with other cultures and fostering understanding, a brighter future could be built for all. And so, in 1868, with a fleet of three dhows laden with spices, silks, and a thirst for knowledge, Omar and his crew set sail from the port of Deira. Ramar, now a middle-aged man but feeling youthful with ambition, stood at the helm of his own dhow, his heart brimming with excitement. He carried with him the family journal, a constant reminder of the adventurous spirit that flowed through his veins, and the unwavering belief that the world was full of wonder and possibility.

The dhow, adorned with colourful flags, set sail from the bustling port of Deira, carrying with it the hopes and dreams of Ramar and his crew. With courageous hearts, Ramar, along with a small group of other families, embarked on a perilous journey. They travelled by land, crossing treacherous deserts and navigating treacherous mountain passes, facing the ever-present threat of bandits and marauders. Finally, after weeks of arduous travel, they reached the coast and boarded a small sailing ship, their hopes and fears intertwined with the creaking of the vessel. The voyage across the vast ocean was a terrifying ordeal. The ship tossed and turned in the relentless grip of the sea, the passengers clinging to their meagre belongings, praying for survival. Ramar, seasick and terrified, clung to the journal, his dreams of adventure bolstered by realising his dream.

Chapter 3: A New Beginning in the Caribbean

After weeks of uncertainty, the ship finally reached its destination, St Lucia, an island paradise in the Caribbean. The sight of distinct volcanic peaks, lush mountains cascading the terrains, and pristine beaches filled Ramar with a sense of wonder. It was a world unlike anything he had ever imagined.

And there he met Chella and her family, descendants of island Caribs, who were a rich history of Kilanago, Taino and Igneri people, they were proud of their island and welcomed them warmly.

Caribs were a peaceful and spiritual people, initially wary of these strangers who had arrived on their shores. However, Ramar, with his gentle demeanour, genuine curiosity and positive energy, quickly gained their trust. He presented them with gifts of spices and textiles, showcasing the artistry and craftsmanship of his homeland.

Chella's family, in turn, welcomed the newcomers with open arms. They shared their knowledge of the land, pointing out the locations of edible plants, the best fishing spots, and the most fertile lands for cultivation. They introduced Ramar and his crew to their unique culture, their intricate system of beliefs, and their deep connection to the natural world.

Ramar, in turn, was captivated by the Caribbean people. He was awestruck by their physical beauty, prowess, their strength and agility honed by years of living in harmony with the natural world. He was fascinated by their deep spiritual connection to the land, their reverence for nature, and their intricate system of beliefs, which incorporated elements of astronomy, agriculture, and medicine.

He was particularly impressed by their entrepreneurial spirit and flair. They were skilled artisans, creating intricate pottery, weaving intricate textiles, and crafting beautiful jewellery from shells and precious stones. They were also skilled farmers, cultivating a variety of crops, including sugar cane, banana, cassava, sweet potatoes, and maize. Their wisdom and sharp acumen with knowledge of medicinal plants was extensive, and they possessed a deep understanding of the healing properties of the natural world. They had amazing rhythm, signifying the positive energy that flowed with them as they moved and the sweet music they made with their melodic voices was captivating.

Ramar, who had learnt to be an astute businessman from his grandfather, recognized the potential for mutually beneficial trade. He began to share this with the Caribbean people, suggesting how they could exchange spices and textiles for local goods such as cassava flour, hammocks woven from natural fibers, and intricately carved wooden bowls. He learned their language developed from the influx of various nationalities was by now a mix of English, Spanish, French, African, and Kwéyòl/Patois dialects, immersing himself in their culture and gaining a deeper understanding of their worldview.

He was particularly fascinated by their beliefs that natural objects, such as trees, rocks, and rivers, influenced all aspects of their lives, from agriculture to healing. This concept resonated deeply with Ramar, who believed that a deep respect for nature and a reverence for the interconnectedness of all things were essential for a harmonious existence.

Through his interactions with the Caribs, Ramar gained a deeper appreciation for the diversity of human experience. He learned that true wealth lay not just in material possessions, but also in knowledge, wisdom, and the richness of human connection. He realized that by embracing the unique contributions of other cultures, he could enrich his own life and contribute to a more interconnected and harmonious world.

In turn they benefited from Ramar's knowledge. They learned about the intricacies of navigation, the art of trade, and the wonders of the Old World. They were fascinated by the stories of distant lands, of bustling cities, and of the Silk Road, a world that had previously existed only in their imaginations.

As time passed, a unique and mutually beneficial relationship developed. Ramar, inspired by the Chella's family ingenuity, creativity and their deep connection to the island, began to incorporate their knowledge into his own business ventures. He learned about the cultivation of new spices, the medicinal properties of local plants, and the art of sustainable agriculture.

He also began to document his experiences, recording his observations of their culture, their traditions, and their unique worldview. He realized that this knowledge, this understanding of another culture, was as valuable as any spice or precious stone. He began to see himself not just as a merchant, but as a cultural ambassador, a bridge between two worlds. The new world he had found was vastly different from what they had left behind. The climate was humid and tropical, the flora and fauna exotic and unfamiliar Ramar, initially overwhelmed by the unfamiliar surroundings, slowly began to adapt. Chella had a large family that was diverse in its make up due to the impact of the colonial slavery era. Chella's sister, Aquene was a beautiful woman of Native American, African and European mix. She was also a musical genius and lyrical visionary. She would write poetry about the natural beauty of the Caribbean and sing her own signature creations with effortless grace. He fell in love with her and as time passed through her talents, he learnt the language and customs and they grew into a new family. Through her guidance and talents, he explored the island's lush interior, discovering hidden coves and secret waterfalls with her and became used to life in the Caribbean. The worlds were a mix of diverse backgrounds and through their union, their cultures blended to illustrate a vibrant syncretic vision.

Chapter 4: Fusing Island Locations with Innovations

Fifteen years passed and Ramar was getting older and greyer yet wanted to discover more of the Caribbean. Before he left Deira, other traders had told him about the first railway line built in the Caribbean on the islands of Cuba in 1837 and Jamaica in 1845 and how groundbreaking this was for the region, a first outside of the Europe and North America. St Lucia, like most of the Caribbean islands was experiencing an economic transition during the post-slavery era yet there were still political tensions on who held power of their land. On a hot summery day, Ramar was relaxing on his dhow which lay moored alongside the bustling quay in Castries. His relationship with Aquene had flourished and his young daughter lay with him, listening to stories he was sharing of his grandfather Omar. Its sails furled against the gentle breeze. His dhow was laden with the usual cargo of molasses bound for Martinique. The family business had grown and today, his boat had extra goods to trade: an edible treasure trove from Latin America and other Caribbean islands– Aji peppers from Venezuela, rice from Guyana, nutmeg from Grenada.

Now a seasoned trader with a network that stretched across the Caribbean, he had a new venture in mind. He was retelling an adventurous story to his daughter Jameela, about a wondrous contraption, a "steel serpent" they called it, that snaked its way across the island of Jamaica. This "railway," as it was known, was said to carry people and goods with astonishing speed, a feat that defied the very laws of nature. He made the decision to go there and then!

"*Nou v'a alé* Jameela!"

"*Mwen enmé sa-a Daddy*!" her eyes communicating how much she liked the idea. She was excited about the voyage because she came from an adventurous family!

Just as his grandfather's journal had inspired him, seeing the excited eyes of his daughter as he shared his story ignited a spark within him, a yearning to experience this marvel firsthand. But Ramar, a man of practicality, saw an opportunity beyond mere curiosity. He envisioned a new trade route, a lifeline connecting the vibrant markets of Cuba with the exotic wares of Latin America and the Lesser and Greater Antilles, all facilitated by this extraordinary invention.

His plan was audacious: to establish a thriving spice trade across the region, using the Jamaican railway as the cornerstone of his operation. He would purchase spices in bulk from his contacts, transport them to Saint Lucia and other islands nearby, then ship them to Kingston, Jamaica. From there, the 'steel serpent' would carry the spices swiftly and efficiently to Montego Bay, where they would be transferred to smaller vessels for further journeys to Cuban ports and other islands in the Greater Antilles.

The initial investment was substantial, but Ramar a shrewd businessman, believed in the potential of his venture. He secured loans from sympathetic merchants in Castries, promising them a share of the profits. He then embarked on a perilous voyage to his streets of Deira, where he conscientiously selected the finest spices from all the traders there, bargaining fiercely with merchants in bustling souqs and serene spice gardens.

Months later, he returned to Castries, laden with fragrant cargo. His Caribbean family watched in awe as sacks overflowing with goods were unloaded onto the docks. Ramar, his eyes gleaming with anticipation, oversaw the meticulous loading onto vessels bound for Kingston.

The journey to Jamaica was fraught with the usual perils of the sea – squalls, unpredictable currents, and the ever-present threat of pirates.

But his dhow, a sturdy vessel under the command of a seasoned captain, weathered the storms and arrived safely in Kingston harbour.

The sight that greeted Ramar upon landing was nothing short of breathtaking. The 'steel serpent,' a gleaming contraption of iron and wood, hissed and chugged its way along the tracks, a plume of smoke trailing behind it. He felt a surge of excitement, a childlike wonder at this feat of human innovation.

With the assistance of local porters, he swiftly transferred his cargo to the railway station. He boarded a passenger carriage, his senses assaulted by the rhythmic clatter of the wheels and the acrid smell of coal smoke. As the train lurched forward, picking up speed, he felt a thrill course through him. The world outside blurred into a kaleidoscope of green fields, distant mountains, and fleeting glimpses of villages.

The journey to Montego Bay was a revelation. Ramar, accustomed to the slow pace of sea travel, was astonished by the speed and efficiency of the railway. He marvelled at the bridges that spanned deep ravines, the tunnels that pierced through hillsides, and the sheer audacity of the engineering feat.

In Montego Bay, Ramar arranged for his spices to be transferred to smaller vessels bound for Havana and other island ports. He carefully selected captains and crews, men of integrity and experience, to ensure the safe delivery of his precious cargo.

News of the exotic spices arriving from the distant East spread like wildfire through the bustling Caribbean markets. Merchants, intrigued by the quality and variety of Ramar's wares, flocked to purchase his goods. The demand far exceeded his initial expectations.

Not forgetting the eyes of his daughter, he expanded his operations and established warehouses in Havana and other major Cuban cities, hiring local agents to oversee the distribution of his spices. He even ventured into the lucrative trade of spices blended for local palates, creating unique blends that captivated the Cuban market. This meant he could arrange for his wife Aquene and daughter Jameela to join him one a special Christmas trade trip.

Over the course of the next ten years as his business flourished, Ramar continued to travel to Jamaica, captivated by the magic of the railway it became another of his favourite places. He would spend hours travelling from St. Thomas all the way up to Negril absorbing the wonderful island views as he voyaged via the intricate workings of the train engine, marvelling at the sheer power it generated. He even befriended the railway engineers, eager to learn more about this remarkable invention along the journeys.

Word of Ramar's success reached Castries and neighbouring islands, inspiring other merchants to venture into trading. Soon, Saint Lucia became a major hub for the distribution of goods throughout the Caribbean, thanks to Ramar's pioneering spirit and his innovative use of the Jamaican railway. His goods expanding from spices to pearls and precious stones. As the setting sun cast long shadows across the harbour of Castries, Ramar sat on the balcony of his home looking down at the bay below and watched the bustling activity, the sounds of laughter and happiness filling the air.

The "steel serpent," he realized, had not only connected Jamaica, but it had also connected him to his own destiny, a destiny woven with threads of adventure, innovation, and the enduring spirit of human enterprise. As the first stars began to twinkle in the darkening sky, Ramar smiled, content in the knowledge that his journey, like the 'steel serpent' itself, had left an indelible mark on the landscape of the Caribbean.

Never forgetting the thrill of her first journey on the railway train Jameela, with twinkling eyes had added culinary flair. Not only had her father built a successful business empire, but she had also played a pivotal role in marketing the goods through creating special dishes connecting the flavours of the Caribbean, with a fusion of the East all thanks to the love and cultural creativity of her father's stories about the 'steel serpent'.

The impact of imagination and entrepreneurism had become an integral characteristic of Ramar's family, a testament to the transformative power of his syncretic history. As he raised his children, inspired by his own adventures and developing their own futures, Ramar knew that his legacy would continue to shape the future of the Caribbean for generations to come.

Chapter 5: Rhythms and Artistry
Creating Waves of Legacies

Generations passed and Ramar's great granddaughter was born, with the name and spirit from her elders, the smell of the fresh Caribbean Sea breeze wafted through the nostrils of young Aquene as she stood on the peak of St Margaret's Bay, Jamaica overlooking the turquoise Caribbean Sea of her beloved Jamaican island. The rhythmic crash of waves against the rocky shore echoed the pounding of her own heart beating with pride of being a Jamaican girl, full of creative talent. The world around her was wonderful. The vibrant hues of the Jamaican jerk chicken being cooked by her uncle at the family restaurant for the large reunion she had returned for, the scent of salt and sea spray, the sweet sounds of the seabirds – all seeped into her soul as inspirations to write, to sing, to draw. She held her great-grandmother's memoirs – one of her most prized possessions. With the year being 2025 she was proud of the fact that she had the original manuscript held in her family for many generations and that she had it downloaded to her e-reader so she could tap into it wherever she was. It brought her so much joy to add to the pages, as she read them and reflecting on her own journeys. She had achieved so much, a promise she had made to herself in homage to those that came before her and because a lot had invigorated her to live her best life.

As she read through her writings, she couldn't stop smiling. Her cheeks felt so full, and her mind had so many ideas, when she looked at her reflection in the waters, she quickly took a picture to capture the image because she knew she would already entitle her painting of it 'Caribbean Sea filled creativity cheeks'.

She darted her view from the pages she wrote alongside the previous chapters that were already written by her ancestors. Although she had read them many times before, the words never seemed to age, and she always imagined something new from the words that were written. Her imaginations had come true and now she could show them to those that would come after her through her literary publications.

Aquene's creative ancestry gifted her talents from threads of her diverse culture. She had generations of Carib people fused into her DNA alongside Arab, European and African roots from her ancestors. The Kalinago heritage was infused in the blood that ran through her veins, a legacy of resilience and connection to Caribbean islands, echoing in the ancient rhythms of the Areíto, the ceremonial dances and music of her ancestors. Complementing this was her Taino ancestry gifting her with a deep reverence for nature, a sense of oneness with the island's spirit, reflected in the haunting melodies of the Ayake, the traditional songs of the Taino people. The African influence in her lineage manifested in the rhythm that pulsed through her very being, a vibrant beat that found expression in the movements of her body and the melodies that flowed from her lips. Her Portuguese European bloodline, a distant echo of colonial history, added a touch of melancholic introspection to her soul, evident in the lilting melodies and passionate flamenco influences that occasionally crept into her music. And not forgetting her Arab heritage, coming from a successful family of Emirati traders who travelled at the end of the Ottoman Empire to settle in the Caribbean.

Aquene was an eclectic child of the island, nurtured by its visitors, rhythms and imbued with its spirit. She possessed a natural talent for the arts, gifts that blossomed in her with effortless grace. Poetry flowed from her lips because of her sharp wit and intelligent mind. Following on from the footsteps of her mother Regina, who was a scholar that taught in the Middle East and North African region through Aquene's childhood and her Aunt Corerle, who was the first Caribbean nurse to work in Saudi Arabia, Aquene had a caring and wise disposition that emanated through her voice, a mesmerizing blend of honey and spice that could calm others while weaving intricate melodies that captivated the soul, echoing the soulful sounds of mento and the vibrant energy of soca. Her voice was a cascading waterfall, words tumbling over each other in a vibrant tapestry of imagery and emotion, reminiscent of the lyrical beauty of calypso and the social educational commentary of reggae. Her hands held exploratory veins, guided by forces and energy of her adventurous family, she effortlessly brought forth vibrant paintings, capturing the essence of the island's beauty in her strokes using vibrant colours, reminiscent of the intricate patterns and tropical hues found in Jamaican art and the bold expressions of Cuban visual art.

However, Aquene's world was not just confined to the Caribbean. Because of her great-great grandfather Omar she was captivated by early stories of the Arabian Peninsula, tales of desert nomads, of bustling souqs full of traders from far and wide. She loved to learn about the history and graceful movements of Emirati folk dancers. She would read the memoirs of her grandfather Ramar being taught the swirling rhythms of the Al-Ayyala, immersing her imagination into the rhythmic clapping and intricate footwork that told stories of bravery and resilience. These tales, woven into the fabric of her imagination, added another layer of richness to her already diverse Caribbean cultural tapestry.

Aquene had a desire to incorporate her Caribbean history and creative escapades of Ramar's Arab ancient past and exploratory adventures from Deira to St Lucia into her artistic work. Regina would often comment on how she was captivated by Aquene's artistry. She was mesmerized by the way her fingers danced across the canvas, capturing the essence of how she illustrated the island's spirit. She was equally enthralled by the range in her music inspired by Caribbean musical greats of all ages like Millie Smalls, Marcia Griffiths, Dame Marie Selipha 'Sesenne' Descartes, Gloria Estafan and Rihanna.

Most notably Aquene, knew a lot about Sesenne through her ancestral memoirs, because the famous singer spent time with her grandmother Jameela and being influenced by her passion to keep the Caribbean dialect of Kwéyòl alive and well on the island. Mirroring her admiration for Louise Bennett-Coverley, well known as 'Miss Lou' a great Caribbean lyricist from Jamaica, Regina was inspired by these women from her childhood days and shared their work extensively to those she taught highlighting the critical thinking ability these ladies evidenced through their poetic and musical expressions. Regina instilled this in her teaching to her daughter with a multitude of brilliance because she wanted to ensure Aquene would continue to spread the history of these Caribbean greats from the archipelago and spread their knowledge to the wider world. As an international educator she knew the potential of creative talent to improve communities, transcend prejudices, cultivate knowledge economies and, to captivate audiences far beyond the shores of the Caribbean.

Bolstered by her mother's advice and vision, Aquene had already begun fulfilling her dreams. Her extensive network of contacts across the Arabian Peninsula, gained from her familial networks added to her undergraduate degree in Caribbean History and International Relations obtained from the University of the West Indies. She had embarked on a postgraduate degree in Language Communications and Artificial Intelligence with University of Birmingham and this led her to spending time at their Dubai campus while completing her research. As a student she introduced her lecturers and colleagues to the literary world of modern contemporary authors from Caribbean islands such as Joanne C. Hillhouse who was an acclaimed Antiguan writer and founder of an inspirational organisation 'Wadadli Pen' which supported local writers of the Caribbean to showcase their literary talents. She would recite and encourage critical debates with her colleagues and encourage book club discussions from works of the prolifically celebrated Aruban/St Maarten based writer, journalist and publisher Lesana Sekou. Through her knowledgeable expose of his works, developed through her time at the University of West Indies and immersing herself into publications from UWI Press and House of Nehisi publishing houses alongside others in the CARICOM region and associated countries, she delighted in teaching scholars and faculty in the university about the history of Caribbean literature from pre-colonial times to present day 21st century. She too found herself learning copiously about the vast history of Arab literature dating way back to ancient times courtesy of works held in renowned libraries in the region such as Biblioteca Alexandrina in Alexandria Egypt during Ptolemaic times and Al-Qarwiyyan library in Morocco developed during the Golden Era. She would fuse these into her creative writing, fusing the old with the new and her piqued interest in futurism that was being driven by her deeper understanding of learning technologies and artificial intelligence. As she sat reading her words in the memoir, she remembered the epiphanies that would be stimulated in her from her many trips to the exhibitions and talks held at the iconic Museum of the Future on Sheikh Zayed road where she met a plethora of futurists, professionals and fellow Caribbean tourists because 'Habibi aljamie yati 'iilaa dubay' - everyone comes to Dubai! She recounted with a smile as she heard it so many times. Her happy thoughts, love for the arts and global heritage cemented her ambition and focus to become an artistic and cultural international ambassador. Through her time in the UAE, she was able to showcase her talent in opulence and style, meeting with investors who were eager to commission her paintings and written work, support her vision and endeavours to fuse virtual technologies into her artistic work. She contacted the owner of one of the most decadent hotels in the country and performed at the 'Q Bar and Lounge', a special moment she would never forget in memory was performing in the presence of its original owner, the late Quincy Jones whose musical impact on the 20th century was profound. As she performed a medley of her own spoken word poetry followed by two

Caribbean calypso tracks she had written with an Arabic melody, this captivated the crowds. She incorporated the rhythmic movements of the Ayyala into her dance performances, creating a mesmerizing blend of North American soul with Caribbean grace and Arabian dynamism. Patrons and fans she encountered, impressed by her unique blend of Caribbean and Arabian influences, gave her an encore, cheering her to perform for longer. Ahh! She remembered with an uplifting sigh - one of the best nights of her life so far! Inspired by the exotic spices and blends from all over the east, Aquene also created paintings during her Dubai days showcasing them at galleries in Alserkal Aveunue, depicting scenes from the Fujairah mountains that she visited but, showcasing the wadis with vibrant colours and intricate patterns to represent a Caribbean juxtaposition to include both worlds in her work. She used saffron to create vibrant yellows in her paintings, turmeric to achieve earthy tones, and cinnamon to add touches of warmth and depth in her scenery. In turn, she would also infuse her musical performances with spices, uncovering fragrances of cardamom and clove to complement her voice, creating an intoxicating sensory experience for her audience as she sang, reminiscent of the aromatic blends used in traditional Caribbean cuisine.

Using knowledge of computing technologies from completing her studies, and gastronomic knowledge from her familial background, Aquene's art featured sensory boards and battery powered Braille surfaces to enhance inclusive and communicative experiences for those that commissioned her to create exclusive visuals. She reached out to the Dubai Tourism Authority with a novel idea, transforming a yacht vessel in Dubai Marina into a floating art gallery for her to showcase not only her paintings but also to develop a space for authors and other artists, influenced by her work to sell their literary works alongside her. Paperback books and a specialised electronic section known as the 'Caribarab wall' was designed to transform literary creations into audio books for people to listen to and adding further Braille installations to showcase written and visual features representing the merge of Caribbean and Arab worlds in the gallery. The floating gallery soon became a highly sought after and popular tourist destination to all those visiting the United Arab Emirates from all over the Gulf region and wider world.

Aquene's fame spread far and wide. She became known throughout the Arabian Peninsula and her gallery "Island Ibis," became synonymous with who she was. Her paintings, a vibrant fusion of Caribbean spirit and Arabian influences, adorned the walls of palaces and mansions, a testament to her artistic genius. When making special appearances, she would often wear bright colours to typify the different colours of Caribbean Ibis birds to signify their striking appearance, captivating audiences with her presence.

News of her unique blend of Caribbean and Arabian influences reached the shores of Bahrain, a vibrant cultural hub in the heart of the Persian Gulf. Intrigued by her innovative approach to music and dance, the 'House of Khalifa' Bahraini royal family invited Aquene to perform at a prestigious cultural festival.

This invitation proved to be another pivotal point in Aquene's career. Her spoken word and musical performances in Bahrain were a resounding success. The audience, captivated by her unique blend of Caribbean rhythms, poetry and Arabian melodies, was mesmerized. The graceful movements of the Ayyala, seamlessly integrated into her own dynamic dance style, created a visual spectacle that left the audience breathless.

News of her performance spread throughout the region. Aquene was hailed as a cultural ambassador, a bridge between the East and the West. She was invited to teach workshops at the Omani Royal Opera House in Muscat, where she shared her knowledge of Caribbean rhythms, dance techniques, and the importance of cultural exchange through dual-language poetic discoveries.

Aquene's influence on the Arab music and art scene was significant. Working with the Saudi based Rotana Music Group she inspired a new generation of artists to explore the fusion of traditional Arabic music, English spoken word and contemporary dance styles emanating from the Caribbean and Arab worlds. She fostered a spirit of creativity and innovation, encouraging others to experiment with new sounds and explore the diverse influences that shaped their own cultural identities. In turn, she was deeply inspired by the vibrant art scene across the region. She was captivated by the intricate geometric patterns of Islamic art, the diverse sounds of Arabic music, and the graceful movements of Arabic folk dances such as the Liwa and Ardah. She began to incorporate these elements into her own art, creating a truly unique and innovative style that reflected the diverse influences that had shaped her life.

She collaborated with local musicians and dancers, creating a fusion of Caribbean and Arabic music that captivated audiences worldwide. Their performances, a vibrant tapestry of sound and movement, showcased the power of cultural exchange and the beauty of human creativity.

Aquene's influence extended beyond the realm of music and dance. She became an advocate for cultural diversity and social justice, using her platform to raise awareness about important social issues. She supported local charities and organizations that provided education and opportunities for underprivileged youth, believing that every child deserved the chance to discover and nurture their own unique talents.

She became a mentor to young artists, encouraging them to embrace their own unique voices, teach English and Arabic, and to use their art to make a positive impact on the world. She emphasized the importance of cultural understanding and the power of art to bridge divides and foster unity among people from all walks of life.

As Aquene's fame grew, so did her influence and passion to empower and help others. She used her platform to advocate for cultural diversity and social justice. She supported local artisans and musicians, providing them with opportunities to showcase their talents on a global stage. She became a symbol of hope and a vehicle to open doors for emerging musicians, artists and writers in the Caribbean and Arab worlds. She conducted workshops and masterclasses, providing a hub for aspiring linguists, musicians and dancers to share the intricacies of their innovations. She travelled the world, sharing networking with other global influences, captivating audiences wherever she toured. In Europe, she impressed audiences with her fusion of Caribbean music and European classical traditions, blending the soulful rhythms of her ancestors with the elegance and sophistication of classical music. In Africa, she connected with her roots, exploring the rich musical traditions of the East African Tanzania where some of her ancestors were from, incorporating the intricate rhythms of Congolese rumba and the soulful melodies of South African township music into her own unique style. In Asia, she found inspiration in the ancient musical traditions of the East, blending the vibrant rhythms of Indian music with the pulsating beats of Caribbean rhythms, creating a truly global sound.

Aquene's multi-genre artistic workshops were more than just technical instruction; they were a celebration of cultural exchange and a testament to the power of music to unite people from all walks of life. She emphasized the importance of rhythm, not just in music, but in all aspects of life. "Rhythm," she would often say, "is the heartbeat of the universe, the underlying pulse that connects us all." She taught her students to find the rhythm in their own lives, to embrace the ebb and flow of existence, to find joy in the simple things, and to express themselves with passion and authenticity. Passionate about educating the world through music, art and languages, Aquene continued to travel across the Gulf, Middle East and African regions incorporating elements of wherever she visited with her Caribbean heritage. Blending conscious words and melodic sounds of reggae with the intricate rhythms of the oud, the driving beat of ska with the infectious energy of soca, and the smooth, seductive sounds of zouk into her own unique blend. She incorporated elements of traditional Arab musical instruments, such as the hypnotic melodies of the rebab, into her compositions. She created paintings that reflected the diverse cultures she encountered on her travels, capturing the essence of each place in vibrant hues and bold strokes, from the vibrant colours of the souqs of Istanbul to the serene beauty of the Japanese countryside. She even began to incorporate elements of Islamic art, such as intricate geometric patterns and arabesque designs, into her own artistic style.

Fusing her art forms became a bridge between cultures, a testament to the power of human creativity to transcend boundaries. She celebrated the diversity of the human experience, drawing inspiration from the vibrant tapestry of cultures that had shaped her own identity. She wrote literature in Kwéyòl patois, English patois and Quranic Arabic as she picked up words through her travels. She incorporated the rhythms of all over the Caribbean in singing her repertoire's, sweet samba to musical ska, the pulsating beats of dancehall and soca, the magic of zouk and merengue, the joyful rhythms of calypso, and the lyrical education of rich reggae, finding inspiration in each unique expression of her Caribbean heritage.

Returning to Jamaica for the family reunion had come at the best time because she believed 2025 was a wonderful year to be thriving in the Caribbean as a creative artist. She was ready to bring her creative, critical thinking and sharp mindset to influence the next generation with positivity. The world, entering the realm of artificial intelligence piercing through every industry and outlet had its positives and negatives, however fresh from completing her research and achieving creative heights she knew she was ready to educate others on the impact of humans using technologies to improve equity and empowerment. Listening to how the sound speakers reverberated the music she loved to hear and watching everyone dance and be in good vibes made her so emboldened as a young leader because despite challenges, she knew that others had the potential to achieve what she already did with the right guidance, resources and collective, collaborative mindset. Her family legacy, one of rhythm and artistry with a vibrant trade tapestry woven into threads of diverse cultures, continued to inspire her and uplift audiences around the world. Her workshops and masterclasses produced a new generation of talented artists, each carrying the torch of her legacy, spreading the message of cultural exchange and artistic expression. She was proud because she knew she was fulfilling her mother and grandmother's wishes, to spread the creative legacy emanating from her family's syncretic roots, ensuring it would continue to grow long after her passing. Her linguistic, musical and dance creations which were a vibrant testament to the power of cultural fusion, continued to inspire and uplift audiences around the world. Her workshops and masterclasses produced a new generation of talented artists, each carrying the torch of her legacy, spreading the message of cultural exchange and artistic expression.

She finished writing, reading and perusing through the previous pages of memoirs which now included her own testament to the extraordinary family legacy she hailed from. From the trendsetter Ramar, a man who bridged continents and united cultures, she too was leaving an indelible mark on the world after being stimulated by the family and this famous heirloom journal. Aquene, a Caribbean descendent of her great grandmother of the same name, was convinced with unwavering belief in the power of the showcasing cultures and human creativity to achieve greatness and spread happiness to others to overcome adversities. Aquene, the Island Ibis, had not only achieved her own dreams but had also inspired countless others to pursue their passions, to embrace their own unique voices, and to create art and lyrical creations that would educate continue legacies. She closed the book revelling in the beauty of cultural exchange, and hurriedly looked forward to rejoining the reunion and learn all about her other family members and their endeavours.

Novelette Part 2 – Culinary cookbook of Friendships, Heritage, and Entrepreneurial Connections

This is a heartwarming and inspiring part 2 revealing a cookbook of culinary adventure, cultural exchange, and the enduring power of family and friendships. Each chapter reveals a recipe to celebrate culinary diversity, providing a delicious invitation to explore the Caribbean and Arab worlds, through different flavours each time under themes of travel, culinary exploration, and entrepreneurship.

This novelette builds on elements from the previous, enhancing the narrative with a broader scope, deeper character development, and a stronger emphasis on cultural exchange and the power of food to connect people across continents.

It aims to capture the essence of the story while enticing potential readers with its themes of travel, culinary exploration, and cultural entrepreneurship.

Chapter 6: Gizzadas in Kunafah

Michroché delicately arranged the ingredients for her unique dessert dish. Her grandmother, Jameela, sitting amongst a whirlwind of activity at the reunion in a beautiful blue and yellow traditional St. Lucian dress, supervised, her eyes twinkling with pride. She had her family around her and was in her element at the Jamaican branch of "La Mer" nestled in the Errol Flynn Marina in Port Antonio.

"Remember Michroché," Jameela cautioned, her voice carrying a stern but sweet tone, "flavour is a journey, a symphony of tastes. Let the recipe you reveal take your audience to new places."

Known lovingly as Miché, whenever she heard her grandmother call her Michroché, she knew she had to take it seriously. Miché already a celebrated chef with a global following, smiled. "I know, Grandma. It's all thanks to you, to our family."

Their journeys began generations ago, when Miché's family, emigrated from the United Arab Emirates and then on to the Caribbean, as commercial traders. Driven by a spirit of adventure and a desire to discover the Americas, her Arab ancestors travelled across the Arabian Sea, laden with spices, pearls, and dreams and set up a life in St Lucia.

The scent of roasting spices hung heavy in the air; a fragrant tapestry woven from the threads of generations. Jameela, with her fiery no-nonsense attitude and shrewd eye for perfection, had been inspired by the travels of her father and voice of her mother Aquene as she sang to her while cooking and this led Jameela to develop one of the best restaurants in St Lucia "La Mer," overlooking picturesque views in Pigeon Island of St. Lucia.

La Mer, a testament to her family's legacy, was a haven of culinary artistry. Her father Ramar, a visionary with entrepreneurial spirit, had ventured from the arid landscapes of the Arab world to the verdant paradise of the Caribbean. Along with other family members, he had sailed across to the islands, their spirit of adventure and love for new horizons guiding their footsteps. They found themselves drawn to St. Lucia, captivated by its lush vegetation and volcanic peaks.

Fused with the talented and wisdom of the Carib people, their family expanded, their artistic successes alongside their business ventures blossomed. They spread their artistic and critical thinking abilities and their entrepreneurial spirit to their children, and in turn Jameela's children and siblings' children, continuing to build a formidable legacy, blending their Arab and Caribbean heritage in this natural paradisiacal archipelago.

Jameela was a young child when her father passed away, but he passed his entrepreneurial spirit onto her and though her early years of travelling with him, she developed a penchant for different foods and possessed a natural culinary prowess. Food, to her, was more than sustenance; it was a celebration of life, a bridge connecting cultures, a way to share joy and create unforgettable experiences. From a young age, she was surrounded by the vibrant flavours of the Caribbean and Arab lands – the fiery heat of Jamican jerk chicken, healthy ackee and saltfish, St Lucian spicy boudin and bouyon, the sweetness of ripe mangoes and soursops her favourite fruits, the comforting embraces that enveloped from the juice that would bring back childhood memories. Through joining her father on his travels, she was exposed to the rich tapestry of Arab cuisine, learning about the delicate artistry of making machboos, the fragrant spices used in making khuzi, and the subtle sweetness of luqaimats. This unique blend of influences ignited her creativity, pushing her to experiment, to innovate with ingredients of her world, to create dishes that were both familiar and quite unique.

At "La Mer," Jameela's passion for culinary fusion shone through. Her menus featured a testament to her travels, a celebration of her heritage. Guests savoured the "Caribbean Machboos," a fragrant rice dish infused with the vibrant flavours of local spices like scotch bonnet peppers, creating a harmonious blend of a national Arab dish with a Caribbean zest. The "Moroccan Tagine with Plantain," a fusion of North African spices and Caribbean staples, was a crowd favourite, the tender meat infused with the sweetness of plantains, paprika, cardamom and turmeric spices alongside the aromatic notes of preserved lemons.

"Grandma tell me about your famous CJ glaze" Michroché asked as she prepared to present.

One of Jameela's signature creations was the "Luqaimat with a CJ glaze," a delightful twist on the traditional Arab dessert she developed after meeting her love. Instead of the traditional honey syrup, she glazed the delicate dumplings with a rich coconut rum jus, a nod to the Caribbean's rum-making tradition. The result was a symphony of flavours, a harmonious blend that signified the love for her husband. She used the flavours in homage to his name which she lovingly referred to as Big CJ.

"Ahh La Mer was my restaurant, but it soon become our haven" Jameela shared. "It became more than just a restaurant and my CJ glaze was one of my first creations because he made me feel like my restaurant was in heaven. He made me feel like I was floating when I first met him so I created a glaze! She laughed. You know my dear, our restaurant became a famous cultural hub because of him, a testament to the enduring legacy of our creative and clever family, and a celebration of the vibrant tapestry of cultures that had shaped our identity. Famous guests dined on exquisite creations we conjured, one of whom was Sir Arthur Lewis. Because of scholars like him, people came from far and wide came to share their journeys and tastes of the world, a celebration of the rich and diverse heritage and wisdom that flowed through the Caribbean.

"Oh wow! You didn't tell me that Grandma! Sir Arthur Lewis! Tell me more" Miché had to stop what she was doing, in awe of learning more.

Well one evening, as the restaurant buzzed with activity, a young man tall and broad with a bronzed melanin hue came in, recounted Jameela. "Excuse me," he began, his voice a mixture of nervousness and excitement, "My name is Ceejharn but call me CJ. I just wanted to say that your food is incredible. Especially the machboos. It reminds me of home."

Jameela smiled, her eyes twinkling. "Home?" she inquired, intrigued.

"France" he replied, a hint of a smile playing on his lips. "Well I was born in France but I have lived in London since my teenage years and am teaching French and English here on the island. I am coming back here because my Father is unwell and he left St Lucia to travel as an economics professor with Sir Arthur Lewis after the first world war. Your machboos... it brought back so many memories because my mother was Bahraini and they met in France."

Intrigued and delighted to learn about how his family was also a global fusion of Arab and Caribbean lands, Miché listened intently as her grandmother recalled how he travelled with his Father, a maths scholar and advisor with one of the most famous Nobel Laureates from St Lucia all over the world. As a result, he travelled to many countries with CJ's father and his mother a model who had inherited her height from her father who was a Bahraini Bedouin. Jameela engaged deep with him in conversation as she spoke in French to him fluently of her own Caribbean Arab familial connections. She would intersperse her French and English and speak in Kwéyòl – the French-patois dialect Jameela often spoke as she wanted to ensure cultural traditions and literacy was retained in her family. "*Mwen té renmen'y anpi*" she said and because he made me feel like I was giddy in love and floating in the air I created the glaze. "*Bwason favoriz-li sé té dlo koko é ròm.*" She said in melodic tone. "He loved this drink so I expanded on this and made a sweet jus to spread on my sweet desserts".

"Grandma that is such a beautiful story" her granddaughter lovingly replied.

Coming from a family who loved to explore she could not only speak Kwéyòl and French, but also English and Classical Arabic too. Jameela lovingly reminisced that because of her big CJ, she welcomed family members and friends from Saudi Arabia, Oman and the United Arab Emirates to 'La Mer' and then took them all over the Caribbean Seas from St Lucia, Grenada, Barbados, all the way to Jamaica and Cuba to experience the contrasting natural paradise which was worlds apart from their Arab lands. As they travelled this shaped her own menu, forging connections with other restauranteurs all over the world and chefs who shared a deep appreciation for food, travel, and the diverse tapestry of human experience.

And so, my dear, this is why I say, "flavours take you on the best journeys. So let your recipes take your audience to new places always. Not everyone can travel "à La Mer,"

Michroché loved to learn from her and like her mother Regina and older sister Aquene, she had grown to be famous and also travelled beyond the Caribbean islands. She remembered how her mother would take her on her educational field trips to all the countries she taught in and as a woman, she was inspired by her mother's achievements. Regina had become a celebrated and specialized professional of great talent in a range of different GCC countries due to her background in health and education. Through all the range of scholarly institutions she worked in alongside broad networks and accolades from Corerle, she trained and validated future doctors, engineers, lawyers and influential people of Arab heritage. Over many decades she taught students in a range of GCC countries such as Saudi Arabia, Qatar, and UAE. Being a citizen of dual heritage she was able to view the world with a unique critical lens and draw on her own educational upbringing which involved global travel during an era where not many Caribbeans ventured in the Middle East regions. Regina was a proud 'Carib-Arab' lady who loved perfume and had striking charisma, full of beauty and positive energy. When she entered a room and taught her students, she raised intrigue and attention not just due to her unique and effective style of teaching and sparking healthy debate, but because of her love for wearing regal tropical colours and her gold jewellery. Being tall and confident like her mother and father alike, and quite exclusive at the time because there were few women like her around, she would be described by her students, patients and colleagues with positivity. Many would describe her as 'say-yee-da ṭūl al-qāmah shumūkh dha-hab' because she was a lady that left a grand and gold impression that would last long after they encountered her. She became widely recognised as an international scholar and amassed awards as a health and education researcher inspiring her children and other people she impacted to be great at whatever they pursued. When she was gifted with her most favourite perfume – the decadent 'Shumukh' by her Emirati colleagues and friends at her celebratory dinner, after being granted golden residency status in the UAE due to her contributions in developing future generations of scholarly talent in the region; this is when her Michroché and Aquene felt the proudest of her and their dual heritage. The perfume bottle, decorated in the precious stones and smooth pearls contained the most exquisite scent, was special to them all because they later discovered that their grandfather's tales of his broad trading connections was linked to famous perfume connoisseur Asghar Adam Ali who developed the olfactory masterpiece! When Michroché ventured anywhere with her family often at VIP events courtesy of Aquene, they would often meet someone that knew Regina or Corerle, or was taught or treated by them as the Arab influential world of scholars and business owners was tightly knit. Comments were often given that her wonderful spirit was smelt immediately because Regina would proudly wear the beautiful aroma of the Arabian scent typifying her *shumūkh dha-hab* grand and gold moniker. And Regina would speak proudly of her family descendants alongside Michroché and Aquene following in their greatness, showcasing their dual heritage talent and gifts on the world stage.

Michroché had inherited the family height and as an international volleyball player had completed her psychology degree after being awarded a college scholarship. Now Michroché was taking her career to new heights. Over her college years she had continued her love for cooking cemented by her love for her grandmother. She continued their family's culinary traditions alongside her sporting fame and was traveling the world as a wellness chef. She had gained a large social media following in line with becoming a known volleyball sportswoman and TV personality because she often wanted to share her healthy nutritional habits with her fans. She also enjoyed sharing recipe fusions that Arab and Caribbean flavours can bring as embedded in her by Jameela. She was inspired by her grandmother and through her achievements as a sporting star, she was able to expand on the reputation of La Mer which is why today she was at the family restaurant franchise in Jamaica, filming a vlog for her feature at the upcoming Cayman Cookout, one of the world's most celebrated luxury culinary events. Her previous features of Carib-Arab food fusions at the Jamaica food and drink festival held at the University of West Indies campus in Mona to celebrate a successful decade of longevity had been well received and she was wanted to educate her viewers on how to recreate her dishes from the kitchen that she was taught in. Featuring her grandmother in the vlog, even with her cautionary tone filled her with motivation to share of one of her favourite vegan dessert recipes: 'Gizzadas in Kunafa'. Combining the sweet, spiced coconut goodness of Jamaican gizzadas (a variation of Portuguese quijadas) inside sweet ashta creamy vegan milk pudding filling, encrusted crunchy layers of Kunafa was a perfect combination. Her recipe combined the rich, sweet flavours of Middle Eastern Kunafa with the tropical taste of Jamaican Gizzadas, creating a layered dessert with contrasting textures and delightful flavours.

Ingredients for "Gizzadas in Kunafa:

- *For the Kunafa Base:*
    - *1 package (400g) shredded phyllo dough*
    - *1/2 cup unsalted vegan butter melted*
- *For the Gizzada Dough and Filling:*

Filling:

- *1/3 cup water*
- *1/2 teaspoon nutmeg*
- *1/4 teaspoon ground cinnamon*
- *2 tablespoons vegan butter,*
- *1/2 cup brown sugar*
- *1-2 cup grated coconut*

Dough:

- *2 cups of flour*
- *½ cup of vegan butter – frozen*
- *½ teaspoon salt*
- *6 tablespoon of iced water*
- *1/4 cup chopped walnuts (optional)*

- *For the Sweetened 'Ashta' Cream Filling :*
    - *1/2 cup full fat coconut milk*
    - *1 tablespoon cornstarch flour*
    - *1/2 teaspoon vanilla extract*
- *For the Syrup glaze:*
    - *1 cup granulated sugar*
    - *1/2 cup water*
    - *1 tablespoon lemon juice*
    - *1 tablespoon orange blossom water (optional)*

- **For Garnishing:**
  - *Chopped pistachios*
  - *Toasted shredded coconut*
  - *Fresh mint sprigs (optional)*

Instructions:

1. *Prepare the Syrup: In a small saucepan, combine sugar, water, lemon juice, and orange blossom water (if using). Bring to a boil, then reduce heat and simmer for 5 minutes. Remove from heat and set aside to cool slightly.*
2. *Make the Kunafa Base: Preheat oven to 350°F (175°C). Place the shredded kunafa dough into a bowl. Melt the butter and rub into the shredded dough until almost all threads are covered. Grease a 9x13 inch baking dish and spread the buttered dough evenly arranging it in the bottom of the prepared baking dish. Press the dough using another pan or small plate*
3. *Prepare the Gizzada Dough: In a food processor, add flour, frozen butter and salt. Pulse the mixture a few times until the butter is in small sizes. Add the water and pulse mix again until the butter pieces look like coarse crumbs In a bowl. Place the mixture onto a clean surface and begin pressing it all together into a ball. Separate into smaller balls and place them in a freezer to cool for 20 minutes. Remove them from the freezer and roll out each dough piece with a rolling pin to about a ¼ inch thickness. Pinch the edges to create a ridge that will hold the coconut filling*
4. *Make the Gizzada Layer Coconut Filling: Add water to a saucepan on low heat, add the sugar and dissolve in the water. Add the grated coconut, nutmeg to the sugar water and mix well. After 5 mins add the vanilla and then after a*

*further 5 minutes add the butter stirring vigorously on a
low heat. Remove from the heat to cool and then dd
chopped walnuts (if using) to the gizzada dough and mix
well.*

5. *Strategically place the gizzadas inside the prepared kunafa
   dough base leaving adequate space for the ashta cream.*

Ashta Filling:
*Whisk together heavy cream, sugar, flour and vanilla extract
until stiff thick peaks form. Spread the cream filling evenly between
the gizzadas. Add remaining shredded kunafa spreading evenly
across the cream*

1. *Bake: Bake for 350 degrees on a lined baking sheet for
   20-25 mins or until the coconut filling begins to slightly
   brown.*
2. *Serve: Once baked, remove from the oven and immediately
   pour the cooled syrup evenly over the top. Let it sit for at
   least 15 minutes for the syrup to soak in. Garnish with
   chopped pistachios, toasted coconut, and fresh mint sprigs
   (optional) before serving.*

Jameela watched her granddaughter sweetly nodding as she gave
her tips to the camera screen.

"To toast the coconut for the garnish, spread it on a baking sheet
and bake in a preheated 350°F (175°C) oven for 5-7 minutes, or until
golden brown. Watch closely to avoid burning. Oh, if the phyllo dough
becomes dry or brittle while assembling, cover it with a damp cloth
to prevent it from drying out. Remember, you can adjust the amount
of spices in the gizzada filling to your preference and feel free to
experiment with how many gizzadas you place among the ashta filling".

Noticing her grandmother's warm approval, Miché, concluded the
video telling her audience:

"These Kunafa-Crusted Gizzadas offer a unique vegan option with a delicious fusion of Caribbean and Middle Eastern coconut flavours. The crispy phyllo dough base complements the sweet and savoury gizzada filling, while the ashta cream lake adds a touch of richness. The syrup adds a touch of sweetness and moisture, making this dessert a truly unique Carib-Arab vegan delight!"

Chapter 7: Salounah Stew of the Seas

A rteek watched Michroché's vlog on his phone while travelling to Dubai with his teammates after leaving Abu Dhabi where they were recently competing at the international league T20 cricket championship. He was mesmerized by her as she talked and illustrated her dessert and stories about her family. He watched and imagined a sweet aroma of flavours complementing her perfume heavy in the air of her presence, a fragrant symphony that filled the bustling kitchen of her "global family table" as she described it. Michroché, the former volleyball star turned restaurateur, spoke with pride as her family watched her create her vegan dessert. Her journey had been a whirlwind of flavours, a culinary odyssey that mirrored her family travels. From the sun-drenched courts of Brazil to the icy arenas of Russia, Michroché had tasted the world, one match, one victory, one delectable meal at a time. But it was her culinary talent based on her cultural heritage that truly ignited her passion. As she made her dessert Arteek listened to her as she recounted what inspired her.

"The bustling souqs where my forefathers began their trade, overflowing with fragrant spices like cardamom, saffron, and cloves, must have transcended into my DNA because I love experimenting with spices. Because of my family history, I have learned the art of making machboos from my grandmother Jameela, she showed me from a very young age, how to prepare this most fragrant rice dish laden with meat and spices, its aroma a symphony of enticing scents. The slow-cooking process, the meticulous layering of flavours, I remember her first culinary lesson to me that would forever be etched in her memory."

Arteek glided his eyes wherever she moved across the screen as she recounted that in between her sporting commitments, rest day journeys took her to the vibrant streets of Marrakech, Morocco. There, she delved into the world of tagine, a healthy slow-cooked stew infused with the exotic flavours of cinnamon, ginger, and preserved lemons. She marvelled at the intricate patterns of the tagine pots, each one a work of art, a testament to the artistry of Moroccan craftsmanship.

Michroché's culinary exploration continued in Puerto Rico, where the rhythms of salsa and merengue filled the air. After a day spent training for her beach volleyball tournaments she spent time with local chefs, absorbing the secrets of Cuban cuisine, from the soulful flavours of sancocho, a hearty stew brimming with meats and vegetables, to the vibrant colours of arroz con gandules, a flavourful rice dish with pigeon peas. She learned to make mofongo, a savoury dish of fried plantains mashed with garlic and pork, a testament to the island's rich culinary heritage.

Hey! He thought, I've been to Morocco - if only our paths could have crossed! Arteek had a deep appreciation for culinary traditions which is another reason why he was captivated by Michroché – he just had to meet her one day. His family, a long line of cricketers, also possessed a deep-rooted love for food because of their hearty appetites and tall broad athleticisms. Jaybar, Arteek's cousin also had Bermudian heritage through his grandfather, but his mother was St Lucian. She passed away when he was young, and he was raised by his grandfather after his time in the British Navy and spent time on both islands as his grandfather was a yacht pilot. He lived between Bermuda and St Lucia and had the best of both worlds. Hailing from Bermuda, Arteek and Jaybar grew up playing cricket as their uncle was one of the island's best players in Somerset. This usually led to Somerset winning the Bermuda annual cup match on a consistent basis and this was ingrained in pride, culture and love for their island and the Caribbean region. As a result they naturally moved into playing the sport professionally and travelled the length and breadth of the Caribbean as talented cricketers playing for the West Indies Cricket team. The cousins' travels with the

West Indies Cricket team was a constant source of culinary inspiration because they loved to try different Caribbean dishes. Jaybar loved to cook in memory of his mother and as a result of all the seven course meals he was spoilt with when accompanying his grandfather on long voyage cruises around the continent. Combining their culinary talent and athletic achievements was something they excelled in. Wherever they travelled to compete, they made sure to collate recipes and gastronomic knowledge from people and places encountered across various Caribbean locations. Whether it be the relaxing Blue Lagoon of Jamaica, vibrant markets in the Barbados, the beach based eateries in Antigua, or being amidst the cosmopolitan population of St. Maarten, each island they travelled to, they fused the national dishes, different flavours to create their own new culinary additions.

"Remember that time in Jamaica, Jaybar?" Arteek reminisced, "Mr Chaman's jerk chicken? The smoky pimento wood infused flavours, the fiery heat tempered by the sweetness of the pineapple salsa." He vividly recalled the sizzling barbeque grill, the intoxicating aromas, and the sheer joy of savouring that incredible meal.

Jaybar, chimed in, "And Antigua? That fungee, man! With the pepperpot soup... pure magic." He smiled, remembering the rich, slow-cooked broth infused with the earthy aroma of callaloo, a true testament to the island's culinary ingenuity. In St. Maarten, Jaybar was introduced to the vibrant world of French, Dutch and Creole Caribbean cuisine, and when he tasted how they prepared creole seasoned conch with dumplings, the creole spices merged beautifully with European gastronomy traditions of pressure cooking the doughy dumplings to perfection showcasing the culinary identity of the island. Coucou was another delightful discovery they made when playing cricket in Barbados and firmly embedded their love for flying fish.

Their cricketing career took them beyond the Caribbean, to the vibrant tapestry of the Arab Gulf. They were happy they were able to travel to the UAE for the T20 and saw many similarities with the

Bermuda Dockyard and Dubai Marina Harbour. It was here they visited a restaurant at Pier One in Dubai Marina and was treated to one of the best dishes, an Emirati fish salounah, a rich tomato-based stew brimming with spices. After meeting the restaurant owner Raina and discussing their own Bermuda's own fish dishes with her she was intrigued to learn more about the island. "I love to meet people from all over the world here in Dubai, there are over so many different nationalities working and living here. You are the first Bermudians I have met, yet there are similarities between our dishes!"

"Absolutely" Jaybar recounted as he shared one of their favourite dishes – Bermuda fish chowder. I add a special fusion when I make mine. I use our familiar base of salted cod, potatoes, and onions commonly used to make Bermuda fishcakes, but I simmer these ingredients in a fragrant broth, adding a hint of parsley for depth. Instead of the usual parsley, I like to add a vibrant burst of mango salsa. My vibrant medley of ripe mangoes, diced onions, jalapenos, and cilantro, adds a tropical sweetness perfectly complemented the savoury stew. And I like to use a meaty Wahoo fish adding a tangy lime juice provided a refreshing counterpoint to the richness of this fish creating a harmonious blend of flavours".

"Fabulous flavours" Raina exclaimed Ignited by the thought of these flavours, "whenever I meet people from 'the America's' you always seem to be able to know how to cook really well". She asked if he could create a special Salounah stew fusing Bermudian and Emirati flavours and as a result the 'Salounah Stew of the Carib-Arab Seas' was born.

Ingredients for: **Wahoo Salounah stew of the seas**

- 1 lb Wahoo, cut into chunks
- 1 large onion, chopped
- 2 cloves garlic, minced
- 1 green bell pepper, chopped
- 1 red bell pepper, chopped
- 1 can (14.5 oz) diced tomatoes, undrained
- 1 can (10 oz) tomato sauce
- 1 cup fish stock
- 1/2 cup water
- 1 tablespoon olive oil
- 1 teaspoon ground cumin
- 1 teaspoon ground coriander
- 1/2 teaspoon turmeric
- 1/4 teaspoon cayenne pepper (adjust to taste)
- 1/4 teaspoon cardamom pods, lightly crushed
- 1/4 teaspoon cloves
- Pinch of saffron threads
- Salt and pepper to taste
- 1/4 cup chopped fresh cilantro
- 1/4 cup chopped fresh parsley
- 1 tablespoon lime juice
- For the Chowder Base:
    - 1/2 cup diced potatoes
    - 3 stalks celery
    - 2 cloves of minced garlic
    - 1/4 cup chopped onions
    - 1 can peeled and diced tomatoes
    - 2 tablespoons of Worcestershire sauce
    - 3 cups of clam juice
    - 1 tablespoon butter

- ○ 1/2 jalapeño pepper
- ○ 1 bay leaf
- Mango Salsa:
  - ○ 1 ripe mango, diced
  - ○ 1/4 red onion, finely chopped
  - ○ 1/2 jalapeño, seeded and minced (adjust to taste)
  - ○ 1 tablespoon chopped cilantro
  - ○ 1 tablespoon lime juice
  - ○ Salt and pepper to taste

Instructions:

1. Prepare the Salounah base:
   - ○ Heat olive oil in a large pot over medium heat. Add onions and garlic and cook until softened, about 5 minutes.
   - ○ Add bell peppers and cook until slightly softened, another 5 minutes.
   - ○ Add crushed cardamom pods, cloves, and saffron threads. Cook for 1 minute more, stirring constantly.
   - ○ Stir in cumin, coriander, turmeric, and cayenne pepper. Cook for 1 minute more.
   - ○ Add diced tomatoes, tomato sauce, fish stock, and water. Bring to a simmer, then reduce heat and cook for 15 minutes.
2. Prepare the Chowder Base:
   - ○ In a separate pot, melt butter over medium heat. Add celery, carrots, onion, green pepper, and garlic; sauté about 8 minutes.
   - ○ Stir in tomato paste and cook for 1 minute. Add clam juice, potatoes, canned tomatoes with juice,

Worcestershire sauce, jalapeño pepper and bay
leaf. Simmer until potatoes are tender, stirring
about every 30 minutes. Season with black pepper
and set aside.

3. Make the Mango Salsa:
    ○ In a small bowl, combine diced mango, red
      onion, jalapeño, cilantro, lime juice, salt, and
      pepper. Mix well and set aside.
4. Combine and Finish:
    ○ Gently add the Wahoo chunks and the prepared
      Bermudian chowder mixture to the simmering
      Salounah base.
    ○ Cook for 7-10 minutes, or until the fish is cooked
      through and flakes easily.
    ○ Stir in cilantro, parsley, and lime juice. Season
      with salt and pepper to taste.
5. Serve: Serve hot with steamed rice, crusty bread, or
    enjoyed on its own. Garnish each bowl with a generous
    spoonful of Mango Salsa.

Tips & Variations:

- Fish: While Wahoo is recommended for its distinct
  flavour, other firm white fish such as Mahi-Mahi or
  Grouper can be used.
- Vegetables: Add other vegetables such as carrots, celery,
  or zucchini to the stew for extra flavour and nutrition.
- Dairy-Free: Add coconut milk or plant-based milk in the
  chowder base if you wish.

Arteek, still with Michroché on his mind from watching her vlog
and remembering how Raina revealed that Dubai was an eclectic
region with vast cultural diversity of people coming from all over the

world blurted "Is the Gulf region known for any volleyball tournaments?" "Why yes" Raina replied, "The Bahrain Volleyball championship is a well-known fixture and people tend to travel and come over to Dubai". He thought, let me just ask on a whim. "Have you ever come across any hotel chefs or restauranteurs that have visited "La Mer"? It is a famous restaurant in Rodney Bay St Lucia. There is also another outlet in Jamaica. The family have Arabian roots and the owner is a well-known volleyball star."

"Well I do know of Adam Stewart, the Sandals Resort owner and Paul Salmon, the Rockhouse Hotel owner in Jamaica as they were recently here in the UAE. Paul has an outlet of one of his restaurants here in the Sheraton Hotel. Miss Lily's is one of the best Caribbean restaurants in the emirate. There is also another excellent Caribbean restaurant here called Ting Irie so please share your details and I will ask around as the head chefs of Ting Irie and Miss Lily's will have excellent networks to know all the entertainment and sporting stars that visit. Also, you have come at a great time as there is a reggae beach festival event being out here because the community out here is really growing out here, in every sector. The talent and creativity of the Caribbean is truly amazing."

Adam Stewart and Paul Simon were both well-known philanthropists involved in Caribbean hospitality. Jaybar and Arteek knew of them well because Adam Stewart and his family, synonymous with the Caribbean Sandals Resorts all over the archipelago, had partnered on many occasions with the West Indies Cricket board to provide accommodation and hospitality for their performance camps and their Sandals Foundation was famed for investing in sustainable projects in CARICOM countries. Likewise, Paul Simon founder of Rockhouse Hotel in Jamaica had developed a foundation in Jamaica supporting local artists and Jaybar's grandfather had been involved in the foundation to provide networks for entertainment artists to work on the cruise ships. Jaybar chimed in "Yes we know of them too. In fact, we have been to Miss Lily's in New York, and I did read about these two restaurants in the inflight magazine' on the airplane that gave very good reviews so we will visit them while we are here – thanks for the reminder!"

Chapter 8: Jerk Chicken Machboos Mountains

Shadur had grand ideas that went far beyond the confines of his helmet. As he sat on his motorbike delivering his last order he smiled because he knew his humble beginnings had prepared him for this huge trajectory he was embarking on. The entrepreneurial young man had secured his dream. Angel investment for his AI gastronomy startup had been secured and he had received notification that he was to be a great feature at the Qatar International Food Festival. He was to be included as a rising star as representations of the region far and wide to inspire the next upcoming generation of rising gastronomic talent from both Caribbean and Arab heritage.

The rumble of his motorbike, echoed through the vibrant chaos of Kingston. Shadur, a young man with the sun-kissed skin born of the Blue Mountains and a glint of pride in his eyes, delivered his last order of escovitch fish and festivals, a nostalgic smile gracing his lips. This was it. The culmination of years of dreaming, of relentless pursuit, of defying the odds.

Shadur, now a young man in his late twenties, had come a long way from the small village nestled amongst the emerald peaks of the Blue Mountains. He remembered vividly the day he'd won the culinary competition sponsored by the Jamaican and Kuwaiti tourism boards from school days. His recalled his high school graduation where his friends Jhenaya, Stairo, Shara, Vieva, Jahvin, Curtis and Mike had all predicted he was going to achieve his goal, he had stayed closest to Jhenaya who was herself a rising star in the modelling industry. So, she was the first person he called to tell the good news.

"Mi mek it! Mi get tru Jhenaya" Shadur exclaimed.

"*Fi real! See it deh! Mi neva expec anyting less fra yuh – confidence ah yuh miggle name*" she replied, in Jamaican Patois dialect, smiling widely.

Jhenaya turned down her music which had been blasting her favourite dancehall beats while she worked out. She was so happy for him. Life hadn't been a smooth road for them since school days but like her, Shadur never gave up on his dreams. They were strong souls with fierce ambitions, and they had leant on each other through their upbringing, sharing the rough and celebrating their smooth times. Jhenaya, had been neglected as a young child after her parents' separation and her father abandoned his duties to provide for her which created both emotional and financial trauma. Her mother found it difficult to cope due to the familial breakdown and rejection from her husband which had impacted Jhenaya greatly yet through Shadur's similar history, they developed a close sibling like friendship through middle and high school days and became energetically inseparable despite time or distance. Like Shadur, they were raised by their grandmothers who had instilled the importance of self-belief and as a result they held their chests high and focused forward in all their endeavours.

"*Yeh man! Ah so wi tan! Lickle but wi tallowah my yout!!*"

"*Tallowah mi seh!*" Jhenaya smiled giving her response as she fully agreed that they were small but mighty indeed!

"*An yuh know wah?*" he recounted before continuing on in patois

"*Mi glad bag buss becah the Carib-Arab link up is live! An mi wi si yuh ah di Doha fashion show! Seriously proud ah yuh Jhenaya!*"

Shadur had been hoping he would secure his funding because he really wanted to support Jhenaya at launch of the latest modelling campaign she was set to be involved in to empower more Arab women to participate in sports careers. Her modelling career was going from strength to strength since graduating. Through the wellness and fitness training consortium she was in with their high school collective she was passionate about developing supportive ventures and to celebrate their successes. Now Shadur was also able to support her and the collective on the global stage.

"Hol on girl, mi wi call you back, mek me share di good news quick an faas!" he told her before hanging up and switching to typing in the collective group chat on his phone.

'Yowwwwww! he typed, *'Leggo! See you in Qatar fi di linkup, mi secure di bag!'* He added a snapshot of the congratulations notification he received from the festival organisers along with a few images of Jhenaya's Carib-Arab link up flyer and included money emojis to communicate the feel-good vibes and achievements, ending with *'wi up deh!'*

He added another one to the chefs group chat he was in, comprising of chefs he had met throughout his career thus far. The congratulatory replies soon appeared from everyone, so fast he couldn't keep up with all the speedy replies from everyone. He wanted to read them when he was more relaxed and would be able to reply to everyone individually, because to him, supporting one another was so important – he learnt that from his grandmother and her friends who would often mention the phrase 'it takes a village to raise a child' So he sent a quick reply saying *'mi ah guh check each one a yuh lata. Walk good!'*

Good days like this made up for the tribulations of his past for sure and he called Jhenaya back to happily reminisce with her about his past years and to share the recipe of his winning creation that led to his success and awarded recognition to be at the festival.

The trip to Kuwait, a world away from his familiar hills, had been his introduction to a new world, a whirlwind of sensory experiences for him. The vibrant souqs, the aroma of spices wafting through the air, the intricate dances of the local cuisine – it had ignited a passion within him, a desire to explore the vast and delicious tapestry of global flavours.

Back in Jamaica, Shadur built on the opportunity reminding Jhenaya. "Remember when you introduced me to your friend Miché and she taught me about those Arabic spice ingredients and phrases words, I used them in my pitch to the investors and I'm sure that is another reason for my success."

Jhenaya had met Miché when they were both in college on sports scholarships. Jhenaya was a promising basketball prodigy and Miché was a talented volleyball player – they both had Caribbean backgrounds but Miché also had Arabic heritage and would always recount the phrase instilled in her by her grandmother '*abq qawiana*' which meant stay strong and Jhenaya would reply '*iyah mi gyal tallowah mi seh*! They interchanged these phrases often to keep their mental resilience on point both on and off court. Jhenaya's background was fraught with financial and emotional issues as a child due to being a single parent child and she would often draw on these phrases along with '*lickle but wi tallowah*' a phrase Shadur would often refer to as his grandmother a small but fiery woman whose laughter could be heard blocks away reminded him often.

"Spice is life, Shadur!" She would graciously utter to him as she taught him how to make everything from run-down to red pea soup, two of his favourite Jamaican dishes. Run-down was his favourite breakfast that always set him well for the day – a hearty meal made with mackerel and coconut milk that would hold his energy levels up as he studied hard at school. Red pea soup was his other favourite that his granny taught him, passing down the recipe from generations before and always cooking it on a Saturday. He loved Saturdays, because she would always sing on these days. His grandmother was a singer who would practice her vocals on Saturday mornings, her sweet voice singing amidst the steamy pot of soup she would prepare from early in the morning. *"Av patience lickle bwoy, good food tek time!"* Shadur, a sponge soaking up every word, loved food and couldn't wait to eat his grandmothers' food because she could cook! He learned the soul of Jamaican cuisine through her and had to move from Blue Mountain to live with her after his mother died when he was very young. Port

Antonio was very far and different from Blue Mountain – his birthplace that held such wonderful memories because his mother was friends with Rita Marley, wife of the infamous Bob Marley who hailed from there. He missed his mother greatly, but living near the Rio Grande on the east of the island with his grandmother helped to heal his pain of losing her. He would often imagine travelling far and wide through rivers and lagoons along expansive seas to traverse beyond the confines of the natural world to meet her in a parallel universe! Food was his love and helped him deal with his bereavement, it would pain him because he was his mother's only child. She was the best cook he had ever known. His mother had moved from Port Antonio to Kingston and had become one of the best bakers in Blue Mountain. She had opened her own bakery, and everyone used to visit he used to recall. She would use natural spices like nutmeg, cinnamon and allspices to create her cakes and buns and Shadur grew up with the beautiful natural senses all around him. So, after she died, it affected him greatly. His grandmother, however, did her best to help him heal through her culinary art and love for music because she knew of the positive energy it could bring. She also had the original cooking skills that she had passed down to her daughter and lovingly taught him the same traditions, evoking and emboldening his love for food. In addition, Shadur and his grandmother lived right near some amazing restaurants and one of the best bays in the island – Boston Bay where people would travel from all over the world to try their jerk chicken. So, whether it be the comfort of his granny's red pea soup cooking from Saturday morning or the excitement of being around many people liming on a Friday night in Boston Bay, Shadur's weekends were always irie and nice! It was through this upbringing that gave him strength and courage to get through his obstacles.

Jhenaya and Shadur shared memories of their past with pride and they would speak Jamaica patois often as a technique Jhenaya had suggested they do often to keep their cultural heritage strong which would overcome their troubles and motivate them to keep life moving wherever they went in the world. Shadur used food to motivate him and comfort him. A little too much at times, which is why when he became to become overweight, she developed the entrepreneurial idea to start a wellness company. She also developed it from needing to recover from her serious shoulder injury which thwarted her sporting career and Shadur needing an outlet to keep him in shape. Over time, the idea was shared as a collective brand with their high school friends, and it soon became one of the most successful fitness businesses on the island. No doubt helped by the fact that Curtis and Mike who were descendants of William Cowper, an inaugural and visionary leader of the renowned island interschool sports championships – commonly known as 'Champs'. Through their history and heritage, the group joined forces and entrepreneurial minds with wide networking and developed a health and fitness consortium bolstered by their respective careers and interests. Between them all having ambitions to excel in sporting, health, education and culinary careers, with many people visiting Caribbean islands, Shadur and his high school friends made many contacts over their years. As a result, their entrepreneurial idea went from strength to strength as they supported each other through their individual endeavours.

It was through meeting Michroché's sister Aquene at a function held in their family restaurant that he was then inspired to apply for the competition he won to go to Kuwait. While there he met Chef Khalik, a visiting chef from Bahrain, a man of quiet grace and profound knowledge. He introduced Shadur to the delicate art of Bahraini cooking, the subtle interplay of spices, the fragrant embrace of saffron. "Patience, Shadur," Chef Khalik would say, his voice a gentle reminder of his grandmothers' words. "Patience is key. True culinary artistry lies in the balance of time."

Shadur, a whirlwind of youthful energy, found himself drawn to the contrast between the two worlds of Kuwait and Jamaica. His grandmother, the embodiment of Jamaican good food, and Chef Khalik, teaching him culinary arts and Bahraini finesse. He carried these influences forward, stimulating him to fuse two well-known dishes of their regions that he had learnt to cook very well over his short years, embracing the best of both worlds.

To present his special dish, he created pyramid shaped mountain peaks of rice machboos and nestled succulent jerk chicken breast slices covering the top. He dressed the bottom of the pyramids with a signature Jamican coleslaw garnish to add colour and represent flora and fauna. An 'award-winning presentation' he remembered Chef Khalik had told him from "You certainly have gastronomic talent young man – make sure to develop it". When he returned to Jamaica from Kuwait, a scholarship to the prestigious Moneague College in St Ann followed, a further stepping stone towards him achieving his culinary dreams. He excelled, his creations a vibrant reflection of his experiences. The Jerk Chicken Machboos Mountain, a dish perfected from his time in Kuwait and his love for his birthplace and Boston Bay had become his signature creation. The fiery jerk chicken, a testament to his Jamaican roots, married seamlessly with the aromatic rice, a nod to his Kuwaiti journey. Each layer, a testament to his culinary adventure, a symphony of flavours and textures.

His innovative spirit, fuelled by a relentless drive and a touch of Jamaican flair, caught the attention of investors. Soon, he found himself at the helm of a mobile delivery service he created supported by his AI-powered gastronomy startup. His startup was affectionately named "A Blue Marley-In," in homage to being the birthplace of him and his favourite Jamaican musician and his love of the Blue Lagoon - a favourite location in Port Antonio where he discovered one of his favourite fish, marlin. Over time, his business success soared, analysing and retaining customer preferences, predicting culinary trends, and even assisted in the marketing of his dishes from the Blue Mountains of Kingston to the bays of Port Antonio and to people's homes, he developed successes as a personal chef across Jamaica using AI data analytics and social media applications.

"So, I'm coming over Jhenaya to cook for you because I know you have to leave tomorrow and to check out your model runway practice girl before you fly out. Let me send you the recipe so you can get all the ingredients before mi reach"

"*Reddy mi reddy Shadur!*"

"*Mi soon fahwud*" he happily replied.

Ingredients for: Jerk Chicken Machboos Mountains
A fusion of spicy Jamaican jerk flavours with the aromatic and comforting Middle Eastern rice dish.
Ingredients:
For the Jerk Chicken:

- 8 chicken breasts, thinly cut into slices
- 2 tablespoons of Boston bay jerk seasoning
- 2 tablespoons olive oil
- 1 onion, chopped
- 2 cloves garlic, minced
- 1 scotch bonnet pepper, minced (optional, for extra heat)
- 1 teaspoon ground allspice
- 1 teaspoon ground cinnamon
- 1 teaspoon brown sugar
- 1/2 teaspoon ground nutmeg
- 1/4 teaspoon ground cloves
- Salt and pepper to taste

For the Machboos Rice:

- 2 cups basmati rice
- 4 cups chicken broth
- 1 onion, sliced
- 2 tomatoes, chopped
- 1/4 cup raisins
- 1/4 cup slivered almonds
- 2 tablespoons olive oil
- 1 teaspoon ground cumin
- 1 teaspoon ground coriander
- 1/2 teaspoon turmeric
- Salt and pepper to taste

Instructions:

1. **Marinate the Chicken:** In an airtight container, combine jerk seasoning, olive oil, onion, garlic, scotch bonnet pepper (if using), allspice, cinnamon, nutmeg, sugar cloves, salt, and pepper. Add the chicken pieces and toss to coat evenly. Marinate for at least 4 hours or up to overnight in the refrigerator.

2. **Cook the Chicken:** Heat a large pot or Dutch oven over medium heat. Add the marinated chicken pieces and cook until browned on all sides. Remove the chicken from the pot and set aside.

3. **Make the Machboos Rice:** In the same pot, heat the olive oil. Add the sliced onion and cook until softened. Add the cumin, coriander, turmeric, salt, and pepper. Cook for a minute or two, then add the rice and toast for a few minutes until fragrant.

4. **Simmer the Rice:** Pour the chicken broth over the rice. Bring to a boil, then reduce heat to low, cover, and simmer for 15-20 minutes, or until the rice is tender and the liquid is absorbed.

5. **Add the Chicken:** While the rice is simmering, return the browned chicken pieces to the pot. Cover and cook for an additional 10-15 minutes, or until the chicken is cooked through.

6. **Garnish and Serve:** Create layers of chicken breast and rice using a specialised prism to present it as a pyramid. Cover the top of the pyramid surfaces with chicken breast slices, lightly spreading gravy to run down the sides of the pyramids Garnish the bottom of the pyramid with a bed of homemade coleslaw.

Tips and variations:

- For a spicier dish, add more scotch bonnet pepper or adjust the amount of jerk seasoning.
- If it is available, slow-cook the chicken using a smoky pimento wood fired barbeque grill/ jerk pan
- Serve with a side of mango chutney or raita for a cooling contrast to the spicy flavours

Chapter 9: La Bandera in Shuwa style

Jhenaya was running very late, she had to leave for the Middle East way before Shadur and still hadn't fully packed and after staying up all night eating and talking with him, so she had hardly slept. Sleep? Who needed sleep? She did, because beauty sleep was important! But no doubt she would sleep on the plane she thought as she sat in the taxi. She was happy for him and so proud that all her collective's dreams were coming together! She had been planning the Carib-Arab link up for months and it was finally coming together. She thought of the idea when she was originally given news of her new contract and finding out Shadur was successful was just the icing on the carrot cake – her favourite! She was on her way to London to meet with her agent and then onto the Dominican Republic to meet up with Michroché who had just finished promoting her Carib-Arab dishes at the Cayman cookout festival and was looking forward to flying out to meet her there for a girly trip – long overdue! Ever the culinary adventurer, Miché wanted to perfect the dish and get some new recipe ideas from local chefs on the island.

From there, it was off to Miami, a quick stopover before the grand finale: Qatar for the fashion show and the link up event – she was looking forward to introducing Miché the collective in Qatar because so far only Shadur knew her.

Jhenaya had organized the 'Carib-Arab Link Up,' originally to celebrate an anniversary of the wellness consortium of her high school collective – a diverse group of successful professionals spanning sports, medicine, education, and entertainment. But with news spreading thanks to Miché's marketing via social media and now Shadur's success it was developing into much more! In addition, thanks to Shara's connection with Caribbean DJ's who had been working in the GCC region for years she was able to market the event well ahead of the food festival. Hailing from Jamaica, Barbados Antigua and Trinidad, they had brought their following and innovations to the region and had set an exclusive trend through the entertainment scene over the years, teaming up with Caribbean chefs as the culinary industry diversified there. Following forward with more entrepreneurial ideas they had set up a premiere events promotion company to attract next generation talent and established music artists from all over the Caribbean and the Americas regions; North, Latin and Central to perform. They were more than happy to promote the event and as Vieva and Shara, who had developed a large following since the proliferation of talent emerging after the global pandemic, were rising talents, it was a perfect opportunity to showcase and empower more female DJ's on the scene in the GCC. Jhenaya was sure that the girls' recent appearance at the reggae beach fest in the Dubai would have been a success and as she placed her earbuds in to listen to one of their previous live performance playlists, she knew that with them taking care of the entertainment, Shadur's culinary connections when it came to food provision, her wellness life coaching and empowerment workshops and athletics sessions developed through Curtis and Mike, she just knew *'everyting criss and curry!'* or as they would say in Arabic, *'kul shay sayakon bekhair!'* The event was going to be great.

Jhenaya was particularly excited to meet Jaybar again, a cricketer she had met when their paths in unexpected ways following her devastating shoulder injury. When she found out about the Abu Dhabi T20 championship, she had sent him notice of the event and hoped he would be able to make it. She knew that Jaybar's travel passion not just fuelled by his love for sports, it was also encouraged by his grandfather's sailing career and networks which enabled him to travel the world seas, Pacific, Atlantic, Caribbean and Gulf. He often told Jaybar to make sure he made good use of his travels and when he met Jhenaya in Bermuda, they connected like soulmates. It was meeting Jaybar that had helped Jhenaya to redevelop her focus in life. He was recovering from a minor ankle sprain injury and helped her to get through an intense and emotional time because her sporting career had ended. Through him she was able to connect with Amelia, an inspirational Bermudian businesswoman. In meeting these special energies, it had kickstarted her modelling career after completing her psychology degree – merging fashion and sports with ultimate mental wellness. As a result, she never forgot them. In turn, Jaybar, whose sporting career took him all over the world kept in touch with her whenever they could. Jhenaya would often think back to her time meeting them as the island encounter blessed her with these energies to overcome her tumultuous times.

Jhenaya's journey, had been deeply traumatic. Not only having to overcome familial trauma, she had to prematurely end her sporting career which added more. Psychologically, she often felt lost and adrift, but protected by positive forces a new one was to unfold. During the early days of her rehabilitation in Bermuda she met Amelia. Amelia, an ex-fitness model reminded Jhenaya of her own daughter, On the outside, Amelia was a charismatic gregarious force, a successful businesswoman with a sharp wit and a contagious positive energy. Yet, beneath the polished exterior, Jhenaya sensed a deep-seated sadness. As if fate meant to bring the younger and older fitness in connection, Amelia confided in Jhenaya. She was recently divorced and was so weakened as it had been devastating, leaving her shattered and adrift. The constant reminders of her ex-husband – his favourite food, the music they used to listen to, even the scent of his cologne lingering in their old apartment, were unbearable. The weight of it all was crushing her spirit, making it difficult to be the mother she wanted to be for her daughter, because she reminded him so much of her ex-husband which created deep triggers of emotional pain.

Jhenaya, drawn to Amelia's vulnerability, felt a strange sense of kinship, probably because Jhenaya herself was a neglected divorcee child. Amelia's story, though different, resonated with her own experiences of loss and isolation. Jhenaya empathising with the gnawing rejection that Amelia described, the feeling of being adrift and abandoned. She began to share her own story, the pain of the injury, the struggles she was facing as a young woman to keep her passions alive while completing her final year of college, to find her footing and realise her ambition that her grandmother had for her to be a success in life - no matter what. To her surprise, Amelia listened intently, her own sadness momentarily forgotten.

"You know," Amelia said thoughtfully, "You have such a presence. You speak with such maturity, so much wisdom and you are absolutely gorgeous! You know you could be a model."

Jhenaya laughed, dismissing the idea. "A model? Me? But I'm an athlete." Jhenaya was not used to receiving compliments.

But Amelia persisted. "You can be more," she said, her eyes twinkling. "Your athleticism, your confidence, your charisma, your natural beauty, you have what it takes to be an ambassador and figurehead for women – in beauty and brains."

Amelia's words planted a seed of possibility in Jhenaya's mind. She relished a challenge! She started researching sports modelling agencies, and in between her rehabilitation sessions, she made calls, wrote emails, attended open calls that were sent in replies and slowly, tentatively, dipping her toes into the world of fashion as she completed the final year of her psychology studies.

Amelia, ever her supporter, became Jhenaya's mentor. She helped her navigate the industry, offering advice on styling, posing, and building her portfolio. She introduced Jhenaya to her network of contacts, opening doors that Jhenaya never thought possible.

With Amelia's guidance and encouragement, Jhenaya began to blossom as a model. She soon began to grace the covers of magazines, walking the runway for renowned designers and sporting brands during the summer and winter break of her final college year, and even landed a lucrative campaign for a major sportswear brand.

Modelling, she discovered, was more than just posing for pictures. It was about self-expression, about owning her own unique beauty and brand about rediscovering the confidence that had been shaken by her injury and childhood past.

Through her modelling career, Jhenaya had found a new sense of purpose, a renewed sense of self. She was no longer just an athlete who had been sidelined by injury. She was, Jhenaya, a beautiful, inspirational woman who had overcome adversity and found success in a new and unexpected arena.

And through this chance encounter, a shared vulnerability, and the unwavering support of an unlikely mentor, Bermuda had springboarded her life in many ways, it represented a heavenly location to her. She was looking forward to her career continuing as a psychologist and had secured a graduate job in England. This is what led to the upcoming modelling contract in Qatar. She had been approached to head a very influential sportswear campaign to raise the profile of women in sport. In addition, through Jaybar she had also been asked to become a sports representative for the Bermuda Somerset Cricket board to raise the profile of encouraging women to take up sporting careers on the island! for the upcoming test cricket series. Her future was looking so very bright.

She reminisced on her past feeling peaceful inside. Reaching the airport, the driver reminded her to have a good trip which made her focus more towards the future. The link up was now more than just a social gathering; it was a celebration of successful young people of diverse backgrounds from all over, a bridge between cultures, and a testament to the power of friendships and connections. Jhenaya was proud to be so closely connected to some of the best visionaries in the world. As she picked up her luggage, she opened her suitcase and placed special presents for them inside. She had secretly commissioned a Michelin starred gastronomy artisan to create a series of custom-made spice blend fusion for each of them, inspired by the dishes she had eaten in the past. Each blend was personally packaged with personal messages to each friend as she treasured them greatly. She just hoped that they would also approve especially as they were quite particular – thinking to herself with a smile, *'one thing I know as a Caribbean is that-wi nuh inna pappyshow tings!'*

"Thanks driver", as she closed the door thankfully *"reddy mi reddy!"* a phrase she would often say to herself when she knew her mind was set in a positive way for whatever was to come. This was just the beginning of a whirlwind adventure, a journey fuelled by friendship, passion, reflections and ambitions and a whole lot of delicious food!

Jhenaya, true to her word, slept soundly throughout the whole plane ride, catching up on the hours of lost sleep. She was awoken by the attendant as the plane beginning its descent into London. The view of the city showing famous landmarks of the River Thames, London Eye, Buckingham Palace, Wembley Arena, unfolded below her.

Her meeting with the modelling agent in London ahead of flying to Qatar was a success, a renewed sense of purpose stirring within her. She left the agency feeling invigorated, ready to embrace her new chapter. She also left with a surprise reveal that she would may return next year for further modelling contracts with Burberry taking place in the British countryside of Somerset England too – what a double win! She didn't think it pertinent to tell them about her new job in England until later. 'I will impress and wow them with more later because right now the wows of life are about to get a whole lot better! Carib-Arab link up is coming!' She thought happily.

The flight to the Dominican Republic started well, but not long after take-off, a child sitting behind her decided playfully to push towards Jhenaya's seat causing her to be frequently disturbed. "Woii!" she muttered, after she began to lose patience with the continual digging into her back. "This is giving me flashbacks to my basketball days!"

The passenger sitting beside her, chuckled. "Don't worry. We'll be landing in the Dominican Republic soon. And then," she leaned in conspiratorially the child sports man behind you will be soon forgotten because "La Bandera awaits!"

Jhenaya's eyes widened. "La Bandera! Oh yes, I know so much about it. The rice, the beans, the meat..."

The passenger grinned and interrupted. "You're in for a treat. I've been dreaming about it ever since we started planning this trip."

Just then, the flight attendant appeared with trays of food. "Chicken or beef?" she asked.

Jhenaya hesitated. "Oh I'm ok thanks," she said, pulling out a small, airtight container from her carry-on. "I brought my own."

The flight attendant raised an eyebrow and moved on, but Jhenaya simply smiled and opened the container. Inside was a beautifully presented La Bandera. Shadur had prepared it for her. "A little taste of our destination," she explained, offering the passenger next to her a fork to try some.

The passenger intrigued, took a bite. Her eyes widened. "Wow! This is incredible! So flavourful and I'm from DR! Where did you get this?"

"A special recipe," Jhenaya winked. "From my friend who is one of the best chefs in the world – in my opinion, and soon to be on the big stage."

The passenger now thoroughly captivated, spent the rest of the flight peppering Jhenaya with questions about her friends. Jhenaya, in turn, regaled her with stories of her friends and their culinary explorations, and her upcoming "Carib-Arab Link Up" in Qatar. Yep, the flight was way better!

As the plane touched down in the Dominican Republic, Jhenaya felt a surge of excitement. The air was thick with the sweet scent of tropical flowers, the music of merengue filled the air, and the vibrant colours of the landscape were a feast for the eyes.

She arrived at the hotel and there she was! Miché had arrived a few hours early and it was so good to see her after so long! After a quick freshening up, they headed out to explore. Their first stop, of course, was a local restaurant renowned for its La Bandera.

The restaurant was bustling with life, the air thick with the aroma of roasting meats and sizzling spices. They were seated at a table overlooking the vibrant street scene, and soon, a platter overflowing with food arrived.

"Behold!" the waiter declared, gesturing towards the dish, "the quintessential La Bandera!"

Jhenaya and Miché already salivating, dug in. The flavours were an explosion in her mouth. It was a culinary symphony, a true celebration of Dominican cuisine.

After their feast, they spent the afternoon exploring the local markets, immersing themselves in the vibrant atmosphere. They bought colourful fabrics, sampled exotic fruits, and listened to the lively music spilling out from open doorways.

In the late afternoon, they met with the chef, a warm and welcoming woman named Elena. Elena, initially hesitant to share the secrets of her family's La Bandera recipe, was charmed by Jhenaya's infectious and enthusiastic positivity alongside Miché's genuine interest in Dominican culture.

"This recipe," Elena said, her voice filled with pride, "has been passed down through generations. It's more than just food; it's a story, a connection to our heritage." Elena patiently guided them through the intricate process of preparing La Bandera, sharing stories of her family, her childhood, and the joys of cooking for loved ones.

As the sun began to set, casting long shadows across the vibrant streets, Jhenaya and Michroché, laden with fresh produce and Elena's blessing, headed back to their hotel. They had not only learned the secrets of La Bandera, but they had also gained a deeper understanding of Dominican culture and the importance of preserving culinary traditions.

Their journey continued to Miami, a brief stopover before their grand adventure in Qatar. There, they spontaneously met Ben on the plane who had also happened to be at the Cayman Cookout Festival.

"You wouldn't believe it Jhenaya", Ben exclaimed as they were standing near the back stretching their legs during the flight, his eyes wide with excitement. "She was incredible! And the food, oh, the food! I learn something new about you Miché every time!"

He launched into a detailed description of the festival, his voice filled with enthusiasm as he revealed how well Miché performed to Jhenaya. Then Miché abruptly interrupted. "Jheneya! Shuwa!" she cried out.

"Shoo who gyal?!" Thinking Miché was talking in patois dialect – how you mean?! *"Ah who yuh shoo-ing!"* Jhenaya retorted.

On that note, Ben, not wanting to get into any mix and blend drama and somewhat feeling a way out of pocket, changed the direction of his conversation to the cabin crew who by now, were intently listening as one of them had recognised Miché and was more interested in finding out more about 'tea' Ben would spill to them. Plus, Ben had no clue what Jhenaya was talking about with her 'shoe', so it was probably easier to talk to the cabin crew anyway.

"No girl!" Miché laughed. That's the name of the Arab dish I was trying to remember. Ben just reminded me. I met this Omani tourist at the cookout who told me I must try the Shuwa when I get to Qatar! But you know what, I'm going to combine La Bandera with Shuwa.

"Ohk I ketch it now" Jhenaya calmed down. She was tired anyway. And so for the rest of the flight while Jhenaya slept, armed with her newfound knowledge of La Bandera and inspired by the attendee she met at the Cayman Cookout, Miché's recipe unfolded and as she wrote

she chuckled to herself thinking, I definitely need to introduce Jhenaya
to some Arabic foods!

Ingredients for: **La Bandera in Shuwa style**

- 1.5 lbs boneless, skinless lamb shoulder or leg, cut into 2-inch pieces
- 1/4 cup olive oil
- 2 tablespoons ground cumin
- 1 tablespoon ground coriander
- 1 teaspoon ground cardamom
- 1 teaspoon ground cloves
- 1 teaspoon ground cinnamon
- 1/2 teaspoon ground nutmeg
- 1/2 teaspoon ground turmeric
- 1/4 teaspoon ground black pepper
- 1/4 teaspoon red pepper flakes (optional)
- 1/4 cup lemon juice
- 1/4 cup chopped fresh cilantro
- 1-2 tablespoons of apple cider vinegar
- 1 tablespoon Adobe seasoning powder
- 1 cup dried red kidney beans, rinsed and picked over
- 6 cups water
- 1 onion, chopped
- 2 cloves garlic, minced
- 1 bay leaf
- 1 teaspoon dried oregano
- 1/2 teaspoon ground cumin
- Salt and pepper to taste
- 2 cups long-grain white rice
- 1 tablespoon olive oil
- 1 cup vegetable broth
- 1/2 cup chopped onion
- 1/4 cup chopped bell pepper (any colour)
- 1/4 cup chopped fresh cilantro

- 1 lime, cut into wedges (for serving)

Instructions:

1. **Prepare the Shuwa-Spiced Lamb:** In a large bowl, combine all the ingredients for the Shuwa-spiced lamb. Mix well to ensure the lamb is evenly coated. Marinate for at least 4 hours, or preferably overnight, in the refrigerator.
2. **Cook the Lamb:**
    - **Traditional Shuwa Method (if possible):** Wrap the marinated lamb tightly in banana leaves or parchment paper. Bury the wrapped lamb in hot coals or use a traditional earth oven (if available). Cook for several hours, or until the lamb is very tender and falling off the bone.
3. **Cook the Beans:** In a large pot, combine the beans, water, onion, garlic, bay leaf, adobe seasoning, oregano, cumin, salt, and pepper. Bring to a boil, add the tomato paste and the chicken stock, then reduce heat to low, cover, and simmer for 1-1.5 hours, or until the beans are tender. Add the vinegar.
4. **Toss the Rice:** While the beans are simmering, heat the olive oil in a medium saucepan over medium heat. Add the onion and bell pepper and cook until softened. Add the rice and toss for a few minutes, stirring constantly.
5. **Simmer the Rice:** Pour the vegetable broth over the rice. Bring to a boil, then reduce heat to low, cover, and simmer for 15-20 minutes, or until the rice is tender and the liquid is absorbed.
6. **Assemble and Serve:** Shred the cooked lamb. Serve the rice, beans, and shredded lamb alongside each other. Garnish with fresh cilantro and lime wedges.

Tips & Variations:

- For a more authentic Shuwa flavour, try to source traditional Omani spices like liver powder.
- You can substitute the lamb with beef for a different flavour profile.
- Add chopped tomatoes and onions to the rice for extra flavour.
- Serve with a side salad of mixed greens, avocado, and a light vinaigrette.

Chapter 10: Cupid's CaribArab Carrot cake

And now, here he was, at the Qatar International Food Festival, a stage for rising culinary stars from across the globe. The air crackled with anticipation, the aroma of exotic spices filling the air. Shadur, dressed in a crisp white chef's coat, layered his 'Jerk Chicken Machboos Mountains and fauna slaw' with slow precision, a nervous energy coursing through him.

"Bahraini spices? On jerk chicken? That's sacrilege!" scoffed a fellow contestant, a fiery redhead from Miami, her eyes narrowed in disapproval.

Shadur, with a confident smile, retorted, "Sacrilege? It's an evolution, a celebration of culinary "You know," Arteek said to Jaybar, as he watched the chef "that's kinda cool! We should have mentioned this to Raina!"

Jaybar nodded and responded in agreement "Common sense to some, is innovation to others eh!"

They were glad to have made the stop over to Qatar before heading home. He had read an article in the inflight magazine about the food festival on the way to Abu Dhabi and were also recommended by a travel editor from St Maarten that he was sat next to on who was going to be attending. The guys were also proud to watch Shadur add his own twist on dishes that were already firmly established. It was the Caribbean flair that Shadur added that was winning the judges over. The festival buzzed with excitement. Shadur, interacted with the crowd, sharing stories of his journey with some basic Arabic that Chef Khalik had taught him. "Mashallah, your English is good!" a fellow chef exclaimed, "But your Arabic, is pretty good too!" Shadur grinned, "I like to learn new things from people and being kind people teach me phrases. "*Shokran* goes a long way, you know?"

A renowned Omani food critic, after savouring a bite, remarked, "This is exquisite. The spice blend is a revelation. You've captured the essence of both tradition and innovation."

A Saudi chef, her eyes twinkling with approval, especially at his Arabic language proficiency, commented, "*Habibi, mumtaz!* You've not only blended flavours but also cultures. This dish tells a story, a story of cultural exchange, of culinary adventure. *Jayyid jaddan*!"

Shadur, beaming with pride, replied, "Thank you, Chef. It's a tribute to the journeys that have shaped me, the flavours that have inspired me. To say in Arabic '*haza shay'un mumyyez haqqa*' – if I have said it correctly, this is something truly special".

As the judges deliberated, Shadur couldn't help but reminisce. His grandmother's spirit enveloped his mind, and her love soothed his nerves, Khalik's supportive words, 'gastronomic talent young man, make sure to develop it' resonated deeply within him.

And then, the announcement. "And the winner is... Chef Shadur from Jamaica!"

The crowd erupted in cheers. Shadur, overwhelmed with emotion, raised his hands in victory. Jerk Chicken Machboos Mountains, a testament to his journey, a fusion of his Jamaican roots and the culinary influences that he had perfected and improved upon over the years to shape him and his craft, had come through for him again!

As he savoured the moment, Shadur knew this was just the beginning. The future, like his dish, was going to be a delicious and exciting one to unfold, a symphony of flavours and cultures waiting to be explored. He had climbed his own Blue Mountains, reaching new heights, and the journey, he knew, was far from over. Like his favourite song 'Three Little Birds' from Bob Marley, he knew he had created a timeless masterpiece that would follow him, maybe even transcend him and his career.

The 'Carib-Arab Link Up' was even more spectacular than Jhenaya had imagined. Through Shadur's win, Vieva and Shara's newfound fame in the region, the crowd was large! Comprising of expatriates of all professionals, talents of various ages, creeds and nationalities, the DJ's completed their sets featuring artists from all over the Caribbean islands. All the popular games were played from dominoes to ludi with laughter, facilitating connections that were groundbreaking for many, stimulating the beginnings of many others to realise their own dreams. It was at this moment that Jhenaya and the collective realised this could be easily done every year – maybe even twice a year. The Carib-Arib diaspora was not only growing, it could even be replicated in other countries across GCC, CARICOM regions and beyond. *'Lickle but wi tallowah!'* The phrase reverberated over and over in Jhenaya's mind sending her to happy places in her mind to ensure there was no more room for any memories that used to bring her pain. Later, a smaller after-party gathering at the villa that Jhenaya had booked for the collective was a chance for them to get together and talk in quieter surroundings. By now it was the early hours of the morning, but everyone was still awake. Perched on the edge of the balcony, overlooking the Arabian Gulf desert, which was lit up by the venue owners, she sat with them all in calmer settings for them to talk amongst themselves. They celebrated their achievements and had much to talk about. Jhenaya shared her special gifts and in turn they presented her with a special gift. A glass ornament of the famous Jamaican Doctor bird engraved with her name in honour of congratulating her for achieving her psychology position she was due to take up in England. She had not expected that! The air soon filled with a delightful cacophony of laughter and discussions, including the recipe Miché wrote on the plane as she shared ideas about thoughts of opening a restaurant and Caribbean community hub in Qatar. All of them together as friends, and the vibrant music of a traditional Qatari band playing from far away was a perfect end to the night.

Shadur talked about his ideas to develop a cookbook. Others in the group fully approved too. Between them all they had their own gastronomy ideas to share. The head chefs of the Caribbean restaurants in the UAE, Miss Lillys and Ting Irie had flown over and had also reached out to the head of House of Nehisi publishing, a company based in St Maarten. They along with other Caribbean chefs based in other GCC countries had set up a large meeting for tomorrow to capitalize on the buzz from the festival because they had plans to develop a niche product of culinary workshops to promote healthy eating and cultural diversity in the tri-island population, featuring Dutch, French and English cuisine with a Caribbean-Arab theme. Jhenaya commented and suggested they should head to Souq Waqif to buy some exclusive spices before they left, complementing the blends Jhenaya had gifted. But! The conversation soon changed when, Jahvin pulled out the domino set! *"Unu chat bout food too much!"* he exclaimed with laughter. Curtis, Mike and Stairo agreed and in unison chimed "Fahwud!" Banging the table ready with glee. And with that, the competitive domino tournament began.

Arteek, gazed out at his balcony views felt a profound sense of gratitude. This visit to the gulf had been an unforgettable experience. It had reminded him of the importance of embracing new cultures, cherishing his Bermudian roots, but always enjoying new horizon wherever he and his teammates played. Hearing the voices and laughter, the tables being banged with the domino pieces, he knew that sound! As he gazed, he overheard laughter and could recognise Caribbean dialect being spoken. That confirmed it! He went back inside the villa to alert Jaybar and his teammates.

"Ay bie! We got good company. Let's jet! Di session rahn d'ere souns criss!"

Jaybar remembered! *"Fettinvell! The link up!"* He remembered *"Let me check in with my ace-girl, she might be hurr!"*

He scrolled through his phone and sent a message; within minutes she replied to confirm she was in the same villa complex. *'Imma get to it cah that's how you know'* He knew he had to stop stalling and being shy about fulfilling his desires.

Arteek and Jaybar had travelled to Qatar with their teammates after their cricket tournament in Abu Dhabi but with Jaybar more preoccupied with personal matters he forgot that Jhenaya would be in Qatar until he recounted that she had excitedly mentioned she was planning a get together for her sports and nutrition friends to celebrate her new job she was due to start in England. Plus, he was dealing with a lot. Today was the anniversary of his mother's passing. No matter how many years passed, this day was always the hardest to get through.

Remembering his conversation on the plane with the travel editor had got him thinking about his own future. He knew he had to think about a life after cricket and he was considering philanthropy especially after meeting inspirational businessmen like Paul Simon and Adam Stewart. He wanted to set up a literacy foundation for children who were living with loss or separation of parents from an early age. Writing and journaling was a therapeutic way to deal with trauma, he knew because it had helped him as a young child and still did. He would often write to clear his thoughts and raise his mood and communicate positivity and strength before tournaments. He remembered being so very impressed with Jhenaya when he met her, she too had used journaling to overcome childhood trauma after being neglected as her mother never truly recovered from being separated and her father played no part in her early childhood. Jaybar would listen to her recalling the emptiness she felt that he never attended any of her childhood achievements, sports day races or graduations and the indelible mark this had rendered which made her want to be a success in life. Jaybar could resonate because when he lost his own parent, it was his grandfather that was his ultimate supporter. He would blame himself as a child thinking that he lost his mother because of something he didn't do right. His grandfather in a bid to help him heal, would spoil him with love, taking him everywhere on his travels introducing him to the best in life he could afford and motivating him to be the best he could be in his sporting career. But he was getting older, and repeated injuries were taking their toll on him. He knew about the benefits of AI tools to improve his rehab and sports condition but learning more about the impact artificial intelligence was having on literature in the digital age from the editor in St Maarten stimulated his interest further. Obviously, everyone was using generative AI tools like Google Gemini and ChatGPT, but he wondered how these could be used in positive philanthropic ways to create support for school aged children, young cricketers and sports people using virtual technologies and AI tools to develop their literacy with a specific focus on championing positive mental health through story-telling, protecting intellectual property of creativity that would emanate. He remembered Jhenaya talk about her friend's mother being an international educator, vastly experienced in working all over the world so he was excited to see if they could connect and discuss more. He also remembered learning more about the work of his grandfather's friend Paul Salmon and the Rockhouse Foundation when he and Arteek visited Miss Lily's in Dubai. The head chef and management there educated him in more detail about the non-profit organization focused on developing how and where children learn in Jamaica and supporting the people who teach them. With this new knowledge adding to his existed knowledge of Adam Stewart and the great philanthropic work developed from decades of the successful family business of Sandals hotels resort, Jaybar was convinced he could build on this within different sports disciplines, connecting global environments.

He recalled the editor mentioning that he was also motivated to ensure that Caribbean populations could become more empowered to control their future with the help of these fast paced developments in artificial technologies and from an ethical perspective, they had to get more involved. Documenting the achievements of Caribbean entrepreneurs across different disciplines was one way to do this. Whilst the food festival highlighted excellent strides that world nations had developed in in creativity and booming travel and tourism industries, he knew this, alongside sport and education, could catalyse new ventures, improve literacy rates, support those in technical trades and develop knowledge economies. He and Jaybar envisioned franchises between Caribbean and Arab countries, discussing how they could create future generations of budding entrepreneurs to improve their sporting, economic and wider knowledge sharing despite the difference in cultural background. After all history had already proven that merging cultural backgrounds if developed with love and positivity can transcend conflict to achieve great things.

And so emboldened by this Jaybar was very eager to speak with Jhenaya.

Jhenaya was tired but excited to receive Jaybar's message. She messaged back immediately inviting him and his team mates over. Her mission was accomplished and after all her travelling and completing her modelling campaign, she was looking forward to relaxing, seeing him and sharing her latest news. 'Let me just take off my shoes' she thought and went to her room, sat on the bed to change her slippers but fell straight to sleep. Even with the raucous heavy domino tournament that was unfolding between everyone, she was out cold until the sunrise had long painted the sky in hues of pink and gold. She did not wake up until later in the morning.

She had missed an eventful few hours because her friend Miché finally met her fan! Arteek had finally found her and won a couple domino games too! Jahvin and Jaybar spoke at length as he was heavily involved in Champs as an athletics director. In addition, he was a school headteacher and they had made plans to follow up on talks about Jaybar's foundation.

It was not until later that she discovered all this because when she first awoke, she was devastated that she had missed Jaybar only to discover the written note next to her which was a handwritten recipe of carrot cake along with the words, 'Carrot cake and Blue Mountain coffee for elevenses, lunch, dinner or whenever you wake up? Let me know'.

She instantly smiled because that was her favourite cake. Her friends hadn't slept and had gone to visit the Souq Waqif in the early morning before the heat was due to set in. She knew they would love the vibrant marketplace overflowing with spices, textiles, and exotic treasures. Jhenaya and Miché had been before on a previous visit to Qatar when Miché's mother Regina worked in Doha and recalled how she got lost through the maze of alleyways, due to the ways her senses captivated by the sights, sounds, and smells. She was happier for the villa to be empty. So, when she saw Jaybar's message, she called and invited him over. The conversation was in continuous flow from the moment they met with Jaybar baking the carrot cake using the recipe he had written. She hadn't seen him for years and they surely had a lot to talk about! He shared his philanthropic ideas and in turn she shared her ideas to develop her modelling into a woman's empowerment wellness exchange program involving sports and education. A business match made in heaven she thought and separately they began to excitedly wonder themselves if it may well be personal matchmaking for each other.

Carrot Cake with Pistachio Cream Filling and Date Syrup
Ingredients for: **Cupid's CaribArab Carrot cake**

◇ **For the Cake:**
o 2 cups all-purpose flour
o 2 teaspoons baking powder
o 1 teaspoon baking soda
o 1 teaspoon ground cinnamon
o 1/2 teaspoon ground ginger
o 1/4 teaspoon ground nutmeg
o 1/4 teaspoon ground cloves
o 1/2 teaspoon salt
o 1 cup granulated sugar
o 1/2 cup vegetable oil
o 2 large eggs
o 1 teaspoon vanilla extract
o 1 1/2 cups grated carrots
o 1/2 cup chopped walnuts
o 1/4 cup raisins (optional)
◇ **For the Pistachio Cream Filling:**
o 8 ounces cream cheese, softened
o 4 ounces unsalted butter, softened
o 2 cups powdered sugar
o 1/4 cup finely ground pistachios
o 1 teaspoon vanilla extract
o 1 tablespoon rose water (optional)
◇ **For the Date Syrup:**
o 1 cup pitted dates
o 1/2 cup water
o 1/4 cup orange juice
o 1 tablespoon lemon juice

o Pinch of cardamom

Instructions:

1. Preheat oven to 350°F (175°C). Grease and flour two 9-inch round cake pans.
2. In a large bowl, whisk together flour, baking powder, baking soda, cinnamon, ginger, nutmeg, cloves, salt.
3. In a separate bowl, whisk together sugar, oil, eggs, and vanilla extract.
4. Gradually add the wet ingredients to the dry ingredients, mixing until just combined.
5. Stir in the grated carrots, walnuts, and raisins (if using).
6. Divide the batter evenly between the prepared pans. Bake for 25-30 minutes, or until a toothpick inserted into the centre comes out clean.
7. Let the cakes cool in the pans for 10 minutes before inverting them onto wire racks to cool completely.
8. **Make the Pistachio Cream Filling:** In a large bowl, beat together cream cheese and butter until smooth and creamy. Gradually add powdered sugar, beating until light and fluffy. Stir in ground pistachios, vanilla extract, and rose water (if using).
9. **Make the Date Syrup:** In a small saucepan, combine dates, water, orange juice, lemon juice, and cardamom. Bring to a simmer over medium heat, stirring occasionally, until the dates have softened, and the mixture has thickened slightly.
10. **Assemble the Cake:**
    - Once the cakes have cooled completely, level the tops if necessary.
    - Place one cake layer on a serving plate.
    - Spread a generous layer of pistachio cream filling over the first cake layer.

- ◦ Top with the second cake layer.
- ◦ Drizzle generously with the date syrup.
- ◦ Decorate with additional pistachios and, if desired, candied orange peel.

This recipe combines the classic flavours of carrot cake with the aromatic richness of pistachios and the sweetness of dates, creating a truly unique and delicious dessert.

WISE WORDS FROM CARICOM/GCC GREATS

- Marcus Mosiah Garvey Sr ONH

◈ If you haven't confidence in self, you are twice defeated in the race of life. With confidence, you have won even before you have started'

- HH Sheikh Zayed bin Sultan Al Nahyan

إن أعظم استخدام للثروة هو استثمارها في خلق أجيال من المتعلمين والمدربي

- 'The greatest use of wealth is to invest it in creating generations of educated and trained people'

- Robert Nesta 'Bob' Marley OM

- 'Live for yourself, and you will live in vain. Live for others and you will live again'

- HRH Princess Reema bint Bandar Al Saud

إ إذا وقفت ساكنًا، فإنك تمنحهم القدرة على دفعك إلى الأسفل. إذا واصلت المشي، عليهم أن يتبعوك

- 'If you stand still, you give them the power to push you down. If you keep walking, they have to follow you'

- 'Miss Lou' Louise Bennett-Coverley OM, OJ, MBE

- Back to Africa, Miss Mattie?
  Yuh noh wha yuh dah-sey?!

Yuh haffe come from some weh fus
Before yuh go back deh!

TRANSLATION:

- Back to Africa, Miss Mattie?
  You know not what you speak?!
  You'd have to have been there first
  Before returning from whence you seek!

  - 'Sesenne' Dame Marie Selipha Descartes DBE, SLMM, BEM

- Manmay-la di't way!

TRANSLATION:

- Didn't I tell you!

Did you love *CARICOM GCC: Syncretic Visionaries in Paradise*? Then you should read *Caribbean Poetry and Paradisiacal Places*[1] by DR. RAONA REFIT!

2

A literary inspiration to enthuse your writing talents and widen your understanding of the Caribbean. Combine creative writing with holiday thoughts and continued education of the wonderful West Indies! This exclusive first edition of this poetic R.E.F.I.T. travel guide will focus on the Caribbean region of the world and it has been uniquely crafted to add to the memories and positive impressions that you will create as you turn each page. Document your thoughts and imaginative ideas from being immersed into a selection of Caribbean islands and authors carefully chosen to represent the region. Learn about the wanderlust of each location, academic scholars and literary

---

1. https://books2read.com/u/bw9Jaa

2. https://books2read.com/u/bw9Jaa

talents that hail from each island featured and become immersed in the poetry and prose in each section. The author, Dr. Raona, an expert in allied health has a special interest in communications and the benefits it brings to one's wellbeing. The Caribbean is a beautiful haven for medical tourism and wellbeing education is infused through her creative writings, guiding you on an enlightening educational journey of beautiful locations to visit and activities to enjoy as you learn about the islands featured. This is an uplifting book, capturing through its words within; Caribbean wellbeing dreams. Read and be inspired to plan for your next trip to paradise!

Read more at https://refitwithraona.com/.

About the Author

Dr Raona R.E.F.I.T is an author, international education consultant and health professional with a special interest in Gulf and Caribbean relations with wellness, wisdom through global travel and virtual technologies as impactful drivers. She is a proud advocate for promoting the beauty, scholarly wisdom and creative talent that emanates from the Caribbean in its diversity of people and through the breadth of all its places.

Read more at www.refitwithraona.com.

About the Publisher

R.E.F.I.T. Publishing is an independent distributor of educational non-fiction and creative fiction literature content in print and electronic formats covering a broad range of topics related to health and wellbeing, Caribbean islands, travel, cultural talent, education innovations and technological entrepreneurism.